Texas STAAR Grade 6 Math Made Easy

Study Guide with Key Concepts, Review & Practice

Dr. A. Nazari

Published by View Math Education
ViewMath.com

ViewMath.com/TX-Grade6

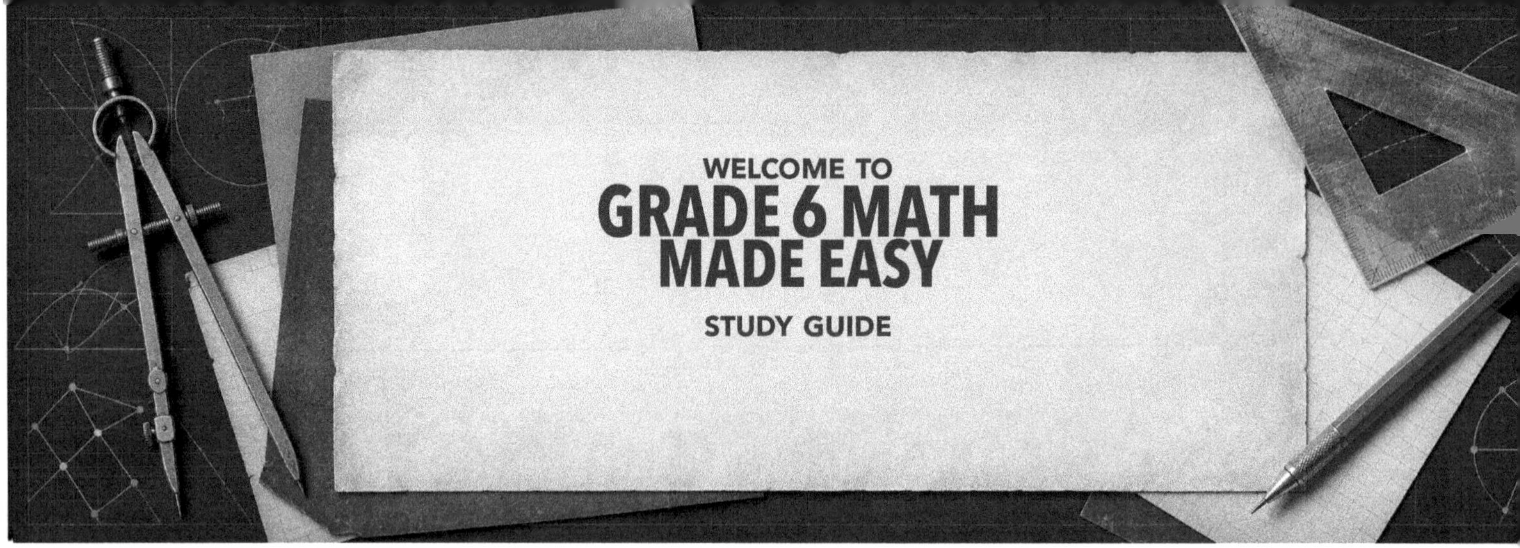

Build a method you can explain, check, and use again.

Grade 6 mathematics links ratios and rates, fraction and decimal operations, rational numbers, algebra, geometry, and statistics. This guide makes those connections explicit: each topic begins with the central idea, develops it through worked examples, and then asks you to apply it without relying on the model.

See the structure

- connect ratios, rates, percents, tables, and graphs
- identify which quantities and operations control a problem
- connect fractions, decimals, and signed numbers
- separate a useful rule from a memorized shortcut

Work with precision

- record enough reasoning to locate an error
- estimate first, then test whether the exact answer is reasonable
- use units, labels, and scale consistently
- correct the method before attempting a similar problem

A focused study rhythm. Read one concept, reconstruct the example, practice without looking back, and check the explanation—not only the final answer.

HOW TO USE THIS BOOK

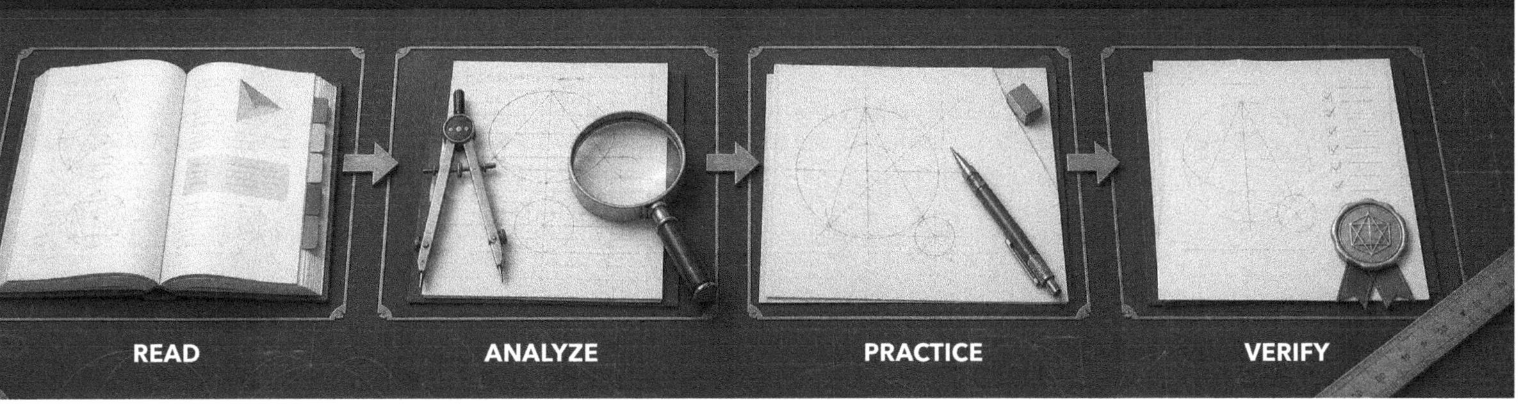

Treat every section as a cycle: understand the idea, test the method, and use the correction as the next lesson.

Worked examples are models, not scripts to copy. Decide why each step is valid and whether the same reasoning applies when the numbers, representation, or context changes.

Read the concept	Identify the quantities, relationship, rule, and unit. State the central idea in your own words before moving to the example.
Analyze the example	Recreate each line. Ask what changed, which property justified the change, and how the result was checked.
Practice independently	Hide the model and solve with visible reasoning. Estimate when possible and keep units attached.
Verify the method	Compare with the answer explanation. Classify a miss as a concept, setup, calculation, notation, or checking error.
Transfer the learning	Correct the work, then solve one related problem without notes. A corrected answer matters when the method also changes.

20-30 MINUTES **SHOW THE REASONING** **RETEST MISSES**

MATH QUICK REFERENCE

MADE EASY • CORE RELATIONSHIPS, RULES, AND FORMULAS

Recall the relationship first. Use this page to confirm notation, units, and the order of operations.

Ratios, rates, and percents

Equivalent ratios: multiply or divide both terms by the same nonzero number.

Unit rate: compare a quantity to 1.

$$\text{percent} = \frac{\text{part}}{\text{whole}} \times 100\%$$

Fractions and decimals

To divide fractions, multiply by the reciprocal.

For decimal operations, align place values; estimate first to check whether the result is reasonable.

Factors and multiples

GCF: greatest factor shared by all numbers.

LCM: least positive multiple shared by all numbers.

Use prime factorization to organize both.

Signed numbers and coordinates

Opposites lie the same distance from zero. $|a|$ is the distance from zero.

A point is written (x, y): move horizontally by x, then vertically by y.

Expressions and equations

Order: grouping, exponents, multiply/divide, add/-subtract.

Distributive property: $a(b + c) = ab + ac$.

Check an equation solution by substitution.

Inequalities and relationships

$x > 3$: open circle; $x \geq 3$: closed circle.

An independent variable is the input; a dependent variable changes in response to that input.

Area, surface area, and volume

$A_{\triangle} = \frac{1}{2}bh \qquad A_{\text{parallelogram}} = bh$

$V_{\text{rectangular prism}} = lwh.$

Surface area is the sum of the areas of every face.

Statistics and data

$$\text{mean} = \frac{\text{sum of values}}{\text{number of values}}$$

The median is the middle ordered value. Describe a distribution by its center, spread, and overall shape.

CONTENTS

A clear route from ratios and rates to statistical reasoning.

Use the chapters in order for a complete review, or move directly to the topic you need and return to the answer explanations afterward.

5 CHAPTERS • WORKED EXAMPLES • PRACTICE WITH ANSWERS

CHAPTER

1

Ratios, Rates, and Percents

What's Inside

1.1 What Is a Ratio?

What Is a Ratio?

Learning Goals

- Understand that a ratio compares two quantities
- Write ratios in three different forms
- Identify and describe ratios in everyday situations

Ratios Are Everywhere

Imagine you're making a fruit smoothie. The recipe says to use 2 cups of strawberries for every 3 cups of banana. That "2 for every 3" is a **ratio** — and you use ratios all the time, whether you realize it or not!

What Is a Ratio?

A **ratio** is a comparison of two quantities. It tells you how much of one thing there is compared to another.

For example, if a bag has 5 red marbles and 3 blue marbles, you can compare them with a ratio:

- The ratio of red to blue is 5 to 3.
- The ratio of blue to red is 3 to 5.

Order matters! The ratio 5 to 3 is NOT the same as 3 to 5.

> *Think of a ratio like a recipe — the order of the ingredients matters! "2 cups flour to 1 cup sugar" is very different from "1 cup flour to 2 cups sugar."*

Three Ways to Write a Ratio

You can write the same ratio in three different forms:

Words	Colon	Fraction
5 to 3	5 : 3	$\frac{5}{3}$

All three mean the same thing: for every 5 of the first quantity, there are 3 of the second.

TIP

When you write a ratio as a fraction, it does NOT mean "5 divided by 3." It's still a comparison. The context tells you it's a ratio, not a division problem.

Writing Ratios from a Picture

A parking lot has 4 trucks and 7 cars.

Write the ratio of trucks to cars in three ways.

Solution:

1. Identify the two quantities: trucks $= 4$, cars $= 7$.
2. Write the ratio in order — trucks first, cars second.

Words	Colon	Fraction
4 to 7	$4:7$	$\frac{4}{7}$

What about the ratio of cars to trucks?

Answer: 7 to 4, $7 : 4$, $\frac{7}{4}$

Part-to-Part vs. Part-to-Whole

A classroom has 12 boys and 18 girls.

Part-to-Part:

- Boys to girls: $12 : 18$
- Girls to boys: $18 : 12$

Part-to-Whole:

- Total students: $12 + 18 = 30$
- Boys to total: $12 : 30$
- Girls to total: $18 : 30$

Part-to-part ratios compare one part of a group to another part.

Part-to-whole ratios compare one part to the entire group.

Always read the problem carefully to know which type is being asked for!

The same situation can give you many different ratios depending on what you're comparing.

Identifying Ratios in Real Life

A pizza shop sells 3 cheese pizzas for every 2 pepperoni pizzas. On Saturday they sold 15 cheese pizzas. How many pepperoni pizzas did they sell?

Solution:

1. The ratio of cheese to pepperoni is $3:2$.
2. They sold 15 cheese pizzas. That's $15 \div 3 = 5$ groups of 3.
3. So there must be 5 groups of 2 pepperoni pizzas: $5 \times 2 = 10$.

Answer: They sold 10 pepperoni pizzas.

Watch the Order!

If a problem says "the ratio of cats to dogs is $3:5$," that means:

- Cats $= 3$, Dogs $= 5$ ✓
- Dogs $= 3$, Cats $= 5$ **WRONG!**

Always match the first number to the first thing named, and the second number to the second thing named.

What Is a Ratio? — Practice

Write the Ratio

A bag contains 6 apples and 10 oranges. Write each ratio in all three forms (words, colon, fraction).

1. The ratio of apples to oranges.

2. The ratio of oranges to apples.

3. The ratio of apples to total fruit.

Read and Write Ratios

4. A recipe uses 3 eggs and 5 cups of flour. What is the ratio of eggs to flour?

5. In a class, there are 14 students who walk to school and 8 who ride the bus. Write the ratio of bus riders to walkers as a fraction.

6. A team won 9 games and lost 6 games. Write the ratio of wins to total games played.

Apply It

7. A store sells phones and tablets in a ratio of $5 : 2$. If the store sold 20 phones, how many tablets did it sell?

8. At a concert, the ratio of adults to children is $7 : 3$. If there are 21 adults, how many children are there?

You just learned ratios — one of the most useful ideas in all of math!

★ 1.2 Using Ratio Language ★

Using Ratio Language

Learning Goals

- Use phrases like "for every," "for each," and "per" to describe ratios
- Connect ratio language to math expressions
- Read and draw tape diagrams to represent ratios

I ran 3 laps for every 2 laps my friend ran.

What does "for every" actually mean?

It means that **each time** I complete 3 laps, my friend completes 2. The two amounts always stay in that same relationship!

Ratio Language

When you describe a ratio, you use special phrases to show the relationship between two quantities:

- **"for every"** — For every 3 red beads, there are 5 blue beads.
- **"for each"** — For each dollar you save, your parents add 2 dollars.
- **"per"** — The car travels 60 miles per hour.
- **"to"** — The ratio of wins to losses is 4 to 1.
- **"out of"** — 7 out of 10 students prefer pizza (part-to-whole).

Each phrase connects words to the math behind ratios.

Translating Words to Ratios

A bakery makes 5 chocolate chip cookies **for every** 2 oatmeal cookies.

Solution:

1. Identify the two quantities: chocolate chip $= 5$, oatmeal $= 2$.
2. "For every" tells us this is a ratio.
3. Write the ratio: $5 : 2$ (chocolate chip to oatmeal).

We can also say:

- The ratio of chocolate chip to oatmeal is 5 to 2.
- There are $\frac{5}{2}$ times as many chocolate chip cookies as oatmeal cookies.
- For each oatmeal cookie, there are $2\frac{1}{2}$ chocolate chip cookies.

Tape Diagrams

A **tape diagram** uses rectangular bars to show a ratio visually. Each bar is divided into equal parts.

Example: The ratio of cats to dogs at a shelter is $3 : 4$.

Each small rectangle represents the same amount. Cats have 3 parts, dogs have 4 parts. Together that's $3 + 4 = 7$ parts.

Using a Tape Diagram

The ratio of fiction to nonfiction books on a shelf is $2 : 5$. There are 35 books total. How many are fiction?

Solution:

1. Draw a tape diagram: 2 parts for fiction, 5 parts for nonfiction.
2. Total parts: $2 + 5 = 7$.
3. Each part represents: $35 \div 7 = 5$ books.
4. Fiction: $2 \times 5 = 10$ books.

Answer: There are 10 fiction books.

> *Tape diagrams are like a superpower for ratio problems. When you're stuck, draw one — it makes the relationship visible!*

Writing Ratio Statements

A store sells 8 bottles of water for every 3 bottles of juice.

Write three different ratio statements about this situation.

Solution:

1. **Part-to-part:** For every 8 waters, there are 3 juices. (Ratio: $8 : 3$)
2. **Part-to-whole:** 8 out of every 11 drinks sold are water. (Ratio: $8 : 11$)
3. **Multiplicative:** Water sales are $\frac{8}{3}$ times juice sales.

Spot the Error

A Common Mistake with "Out Of" **A sports team wins 4 out of every 7 games.**

~~The ratio of wins to losses is $4 : 7$.~~ $\longrightarrow$ ________________

What went wrong? "4 out of 7" is a **part-to-whole** ratio. The team wins 4 and loses $7 - 4 = 3$.

The correct ratio of wins to losses is $4 : 3$.

Using Ratio Language — Practice

Translate Words to Ratios

1. A pet shelter has 6 cats **for every** 5 dogs. Write the ratio of cats to dogs.
2. A student reads 4 pages **per** minute. Write the ratio of pages to minutes.
3. In a trail mix, 3 **out of** every 8 pieces are raisins. Write the ratio of raisins to total pieces.
4. In the trail mix from Problem 3, what is the ratio of raisins to non-raisins?

Tape Diagrams

5. The ratio of boys to girls on a bus is $3 : 5$. There are 40 students total. How many boys are on the bus?
6. A farmer plants corn and beans in a ratio of $4 : 1$. If the farmer plants 60 rows total, how many rows are corn?

Apply It

7. Write a real-world situation that matches the ratio $2 : 7$.
8. A coach keeps a ratio of 5 practice days **for every** 1 game day. In a 24-day period, how many are practice days and how many are game days?

You're speaking the language of ratios like a pro!

1.3 What Is a Rate?

What Is a Rate?

Learning Goals

- Understand that a rate compares two quantities with different units
- Identify the units in a rate
- Write rates clearly using "per" language

Rates Rule Your Life

You probably already think about rates every day:

- Your phone plan: 5 GB **per** month
- A road trip: 65 miles **per** hour
- Grocery shopping: $2.50 **per** pound of chicken
- Your favorite game: 120 points **per** level

Every time you see the word "per," you're looking at a rate!

What Is a Rate?

A **rate** is a special kind of ratio that compares two quantities measured in **different units**.

Example	Quantity 1	Quantity 2
300 miles in 5 hours	miles	hours
$12 for 4 sandwiches	dollars	sandwiches
150 words in 3 minutes	words	minutes

If both quantities use the SAME unit (like 3 boys to 5 girls — both are people), it's just a ratio. If the units are DIFFERENT, it's a rate.

Ratio	Rate
Compares quantities with the **same** or similar units. Examples: • 3 cats to 5 dogs • 12 boys to 18 girls • 2 wins to 1 loss	Compares quantities with **different** units. Examples: • $15 per hour • 60 miles per hour • 3 apples per bag

> *Here's a quick test: if you can say "per" between the two quantities and it makes sense, it's a rate! "Miles per hour" — yep, that's a rate.*

Identifying Rates

Which of the following are rates? Identify the two units in each rate.

1. 5 red cards to 3 blue cards

2. 240 heartbeats in 4 minutes
3. \$36 for 9 gallons of gas
4. 7 boys out of 20 students

Solution:

1. **Not a rate** — both are cards (same type of unit). This is a ratio.
2. **Rate** — heartbeats and minutes are different units. Rate: 240 heartbeats per 4 minutes.
3. **Rate** — dollars and gallons are different units. Rate: \$36 per 9 gallons.
4. **Not a rate** — boys and students are the same type (people). This is a part-to-whole ratio.

Writing Rates

A printer prints 120 pages in 8 minutes. Write this as a rate.

Solution:

1. Identify the quantities and their units: 120 pages, 8 minutes.
2. Write the rate with "per": 120 pages per 8 minutes, or 120 pages/8 minutes.
3. As a fraction: $\frac{120 \text{ pages}}{8 \text{ minutes}}$.

Answer: $\frac{120 \text{ pages}}{8 \text{ minutes}}$ **or 120 pages per 8 minutes**

TIP

Always include the units when you write a rate. Writing just "120 to 8" loses the meaning. Writing "120 pages per 8 minutes" tells the whole story.

How to Write a Rate

1. Identify the two quantities and their units.
2. Check that the units are **different** (that's what makes it a rate).
3. Write the rate using "per" or as a fraction with units.

What Is a Rate? — Practice

Rate or Ratio?

Decide whether each situation describes a **rate** or a **ratio**. Write "Rate" or "Ratio."

1. 5 touchdowns in 3 games
2. 4 red shirts to 6 blue shirts
3. 200 calories in 1 granola bar
4. 9 girls out of 15 students

Write the Rate

5. A car travels 180 miles in 3 hours. Write this as a rate with units.
6. A factory makes 500 toys in 4 days. Write this as a rate with units.

Apply It

7. A runner completes 6 laps in 12 minutes. A cyclist completes 6 laps in 8 minutes. Who is faster? Explain using rates.
8. Name a real-life rate you used or saw today. Write it with units.

You can spot rates everywhere now — that's a skill worth having!

1.4 Finding the Unit Rate

Learning Goals

- Find a unit rate by dividing so the second quantity is 1
- Use unit rates to compare prices and find the best deal
- Apply unit rates to real-life financial decisions

What Is a Unit Rate?

A **unit rate** tells you how much of something for **one** unit.

- $\$12$ for 4 drinks $\rightarrow$ $\$3$ **per** 1 **drink** (unit rate)
- 150 miles in 3 hours $\rightarrow$ 50 **miles per** 1 **hour** (unit rate)

To find a unit rate,

divide both numbers so the second one becomes 1.

Unit Pricing at the Store

A family is grocery shopping. Brand A sells 6 granola bars for $\$5.10$. Brand B sells 8 bars for $\$6.00$. Which is the better deal?

Solution:

1. Brand A: $\$5.10 \div 6 = \$0.85$ per bar.

2. Brand B: $\$6.00 \div 8 = \$0.75$ per bar.
3. Compare: $\$0.75 < \$0.85$.

Answer: Brand B is cheaper at $\$0.75$ per bar.

"Smart shoppers use unit prices! Check the small label on the store shelf — it often shows the unit price for you."

Watch Out!

Watch the order! "Dollars **per** item" means divide dollars BY items. The word after "per" is what becomes 1.

Unit Rate Practice

Find the Unit Rate

1. A phone plan charges $45 for 3 months. What is the cost per month?
2. A car uses 8 gallons of gas for 240 miles. Find the miles per gallon.
3. Ravi earns $56 for 7 hours of mowing lawns. What is his hourly rate?

Compare Prices

4. A 12-pack of juice costs $5.40. A 20-pack costs $8.00. Which pack has the lower unit price?
5. Streaming Service A costs $108 per year. Service B costs $10 per month. Which is cheaper per month?
6. A family compares two cell plans. Plan X charges $150 for 5 lines. Plan Y charges $200 for 8 lines. Which plan costs less per line?

1.5 Tables of Equivalent Ratios

Tables of Equivalent Ratios

Learning Goals

- Build ratio tables by multiplying or dividing both quantities
- Use ratio tables to find missing values
- Understand that equivalent ratios form the same relationship

If making 1 batch of lemonade requires 2 cups of lemon juice and 5 cups of water, how much do I need for 4 batches?

Just multiply both amounts by 4!

Exactly! And a **ratio table** organizes all those equivalent amounts in one place.

Equivalent Ratios

Two ratios are **equivalent** if you can multiply (or divide) both parts of one ratio by the same number to get the other.

$$2:5 \quad \longrightarrow \quad \times 3 \quad \longrightarrow \quad 6:15$$

So $2:5$ and $6:15$ are equivalent ratios. They represent the same relationship.

Multiplying or dividing both parts of a ratio by the same nonzero number gives an equivalent ratio.

Ratio Tables

A **ratio table** lists pairs of numbers that all share the same ratio. You build one by multiplying (or dividing) both columns by the same number.

Lemonade recipe: 2 cups lemon juice for every 5 cups water.

Lemon Juice (cups)	Water (cups)
2	5
4	10
6	15
8	20
10	25

Every row shows an equivalent ratio: $2:5 = 4:10 = 6:15 = 8:20 = 10:25$.

How to Build a Ratio Table

1. Start with the given ratio.
2. Multiply **both** values by $2, 3, 4, \ldots$ to find more equivalent ratios.
3. To go backward (smaller values), divide both by the same number.
4. To find a specific missing value, figure out the multiplier from the column you know.

Finding Missing Values in a Ratio Table

Complete the ratio table.

Pencils	Erasers
3	2
9	?
?	10
18	?

Solution:

1. Row 2: Pencils went from 3 to 9, so we multiplied by 3. Erasers: $2 \times 3 = 6$.
2. Row 3: Erasers went from 2 to 10, so we multiplied by 5. Pencils: $3 \times 5 = 15$.
3. Row 4: Pencils went from 3 to 18, so we multiplied by 6. Erasers: $2 \times 6 = 12$.

Pencils	Erasers	Multiplier
3	2	$\times 1$
9	6	$\times 3$
15	10	$\times 5$
18	12	$\times 6$

"Think of a ratio table as a recipe scaler. You're making the same recipe — just in bigger or smaller batches!"

Using a Ratio Table to Solve a Problem

A store sells notebooks in packs. The ratio of blue notebooks to red notebooks is $4:3$. If you buy 20 blue notebooks, how many red notebooks do you get?

Solution:

Build a ratio table:

Blue	Red
4	3
8	6
12	9
16	12
20	15

Or use the shortcut: $20 \div 4 = 5$, so we multiplied by 5. Red $= 3 \times 5 = 15$.

Answer: You get 15 red notebooks.

Watch Out!

A common mistake is to add the same number to both parts instead of **multiplying**.

$3:5 \xrightarrow{+3} 6:8$ **WRONG!** $6:8$ is NOT equivalent to $3:5$.

$3:5 \xrightarrow{\times 2} 6:10$ ✓ This is correct!

Tables of Equivalent Ratios — Practice

Complete the Table

1. Complete the ratio table for the ratio $5 : 2$.

A	B
5	2
10	______
______	8
25	______

2. Complete the ratio table for the ratio $7 : 3$.

X	Y
7	3
14	______
______	12
35	______

Equivalent or Not?

3. Are $6 : 9$ and $14 : 21$ equivalent ratios? Explain.

4. Are $5 : 8$ and $15 : 20$ equivalent ratios? Explain.

Apply It

5. A smoothie recipe uses fruit and yogurt in a $3 : 2$ ratio. If you use 12 cups of fruit, how many cups of yogurt do you need?

6. A class has a boy-to-girl ratio of $5 : 7$. If there are 35 girls, how many students are in the class total?

7. A painter mixes blue and white paint in a $2 : 9$ ratio. She needs 33 total cups of paint. How many cups of each color does she need?

Ratio tables are one of your most powerful tools — use them!

1.6 Graphing Ratios

Learning Goals

- Plot ratio pairs as points on a coordinate plane
- Recognize that equivalent ratios form a straight line through the origin
- Use a graph to find missing values

From Table to Graph

You can turn a ratio table into a graph. Each row becomes a point (x, y).

If $y = 3x$, the points are $(1, 3)$, $(2, 6)$, $(3, 9)$, $(4, 12)$.
All these points line up in a straight line through $(0, 0)$.

Equivalent ratios always make a straight line through the origin $(0, 0)$.

Plot and Predict

Juice costs \$2 per bottle. Make a table and graph for $1–4$ bottles. How much for 5 bottles?

Solution:

1. Table: $(1, 2)$, $(2, 4)$, $(3, 6)$, $(4, 8)$.
2. Plot these points. They form a straight line.

3. Extend the line to $x = 5$. Read $y = 10$.

Answer: 5 **bottles cost** $\$10$.

"If your points don't line up, double-check your table. Equivalent ratios ***always*** *make a straight line!"*

Graphing Practice

Plot and Answer

1. A car goes 30 miles each hour. List the four points you would plot for hours 1 through 4.

2. Does the point $(3,9)$ belong on the graph of the ratio $1:3$?

3. The points $(2,5)$ and $(4,10)$ are on a line. What is the ratio?

Think Deeper

4. Two ratio graphs both go through the origin. Line A goes through $(1,4)$. Line B goes through $(1,3)$. Which line is steeper?

5. A graph of equivalent ratios can be a curved line. True ○ False ○

1.7 What Is a Percent?

Learning Goals

- Understand that percent means "per 100"
- Convert between percents, fractions, and decimals
- Apply percents to sales tax, discounts, and tips

Percent means "per 100." The symbol % means "out of 100."

Percents, Fractions, and Decimals

All three show parts of a whole:

Percent	Fraction	Decimal
25%	$\frac{25}{100} = \frac{1}{4}$	0.25
50%	$\frac{50}{100} = \frac{1}{2}$	0.50
75%	$\frac{75}{100} = \frac{3}{4}$	0.75

To convert a percent to a decimal, divide by 100 (move the decimal point two places left).

A percent is really a **ratio**: $25\% = 25 : 100 = 1 : 4$. Any percent problem is a proportion!

Percents in Everyday Money

Sales Tax:

A shirt costs $\$40$ and the sales tax is 8%. How much tax do you pay?

Tax $= 0.08 \times \$40 = \$3.20$.

Answer: Tax is $\$3.20$

Discount:

The same shirt is 25% off. How much do you save?

Savings $= 0.25 \times \$40 = \$10$.

Answer: You save $\$10$

TIP

Think of 10% as the anchor: 10% of $\$40$ is $\$4$. Double it for 20% ($\$8$). Halve it for 5% ($\$2$). Build any percent from 10%!

Percent Practice

Convert

1. Write 60% as a fraction and a decimal.
2. Write 0.15 as a percent.
3. Write $\frac{3}{4}$ as a percent.

Money Applications

4. A video game costs \$50. Sales tax is 6%. What is the total cost?
5. A meal costs \$25. You want to leave a 20% tip. How much is the tip?
6. A backpack is \$60 with a 30% off coupon. What is the sale price?

1.8 Solving Percent Problems

Learning Goals

- Find a percent of a number (e.g., 30% of 50)
- Calculate sales tax, tips, and discounts
- Understand simple interest using $I = P \times r \times t$

Finding a Percent of a Number

To find a percent of a number, **multiply**.

Part = Percent × Whole

Write the percent as a decimal or fraction first:

- 20% of $60 \rightarrow 0.20 \times 60 = 12$
- 25% of $80 \rightarrow \frac{1}{4} \times 80 = 20$

Pick whichever form (decimal or fraction) makes the math easiest.

Money in Real Life

Sales Tax:

A video game costs $\$40$. The tax rate is 8.25%. What is the total cost?

Tax $= 0.0825 \times \$40 = \$3.30$. Total $= \$40 + \$3.30 = \$43.30$.

Tip:

A family's restaurant bill is $\$60$. They leave a 15% tip. How much tip?

Tip $= 0.15 \times \$60 = \$9$.

Answer: Tip is $\$9$

Discount:

A $\$25$ shirt is 20% off. What is the sale price?

Discount $= 0.20 \times \$25 = \$5$. Sale price $= \$25 - \$5 = \$20$.

Simple Interest (Preview)

Banks pay you interest for saving money. The formula is:

$$I = P \times r \times t$$

I = interest earned, P = principal (starting amount), r = rate (as a decimal), t = time (in years).

Example: You save $\$500$ at 4% for 2 years. $I = 500 \times 0.04 \times 2 = \$40$.

> *Quick check — 10% is always one-tenth. 10% of $\$80$ is $\$8$. Double it for 20% ($\$16$)!*

Percent and Money Practice

Tax, Tip, and Discount

1. A meal costs $\$35$. The tax rate is 6%. What is the tax amount?

2. You want to tip 20% on a $\$45$ dinner. How much is the tip?

3. A $\$60$ jacket is 30% off. What is the sale price?

Simple Interest

4. You put $\$200$ in a savings account at 5% per year for 3 years. How much interest do you earn?

5. A store marks up shoes by 40%. The wholesale price is $\$50$. What is the selling price?

6. Grandma gives you $\$1{,}000$ for a savings bond earning 3% per year for 5 years. How much interest will you earn?

1.9 Solving Rate and Ratio Word Problems

Learning Goals

- Choose the right tool (tables, tape diagrams, equations) to solve ratio problems
- Show clear reasoning with units and steps
- Solve multi-step rate and ratio problems

Pick a Strategy

You now have several tools. Pick the one that fits:

- **Ratio table** — great when you need to scale up or down step by step.
- **Tape diagram** — great for part-to-part or part-to-whole problems.
- **Unit rate** — great when you need "how much for one?"
- **Equation** — great when you can set up equal ratios: $\frac{a}{b} = \frac{c}{d}$.

Ratio Table Strategy

A recipe makes 12 cookies using 2 eggs. How many eggs to make 42 cookies?

Solution:

1. Unit rate: $12 \div 2 = 6$ cookies per egg.
2. $42 \div 6 = 7$ eggs.

Answer: 7 eggs

Tape Diagram Strategy

Boys and girls are in a $3:5$ ratio. There are 40 students. How many boys?

Boys:

Girls:

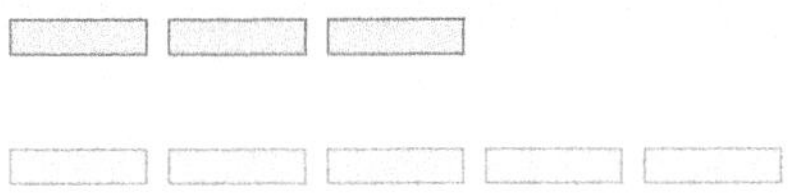

Total parts: $3+5=8$.

Each part: $40 \div 8 = 5$.

Boys: $3 \times 5 = 15$.

Answer: 15 boys

TIP

Always write your units! "7" alone is unclear. "7 eggs" is a complete answer.

Word Problem Practice

1. A car travels 180 miles in 3 hours. At the same rate, how far will it go in 7 hours?

2. A paint mix uses red and white in a $2:7$ ratio. You need 36 cups total. How much red? How much white?

3. Three friends share a prize in a $1:2:3$ ratio. The prize is $\$120$. How much does each person get?

4. A map scale says 1 cm $=5$ km. Two cities are 8 cm apart on the map. What is the real distance?

5. A garden uses 3 bags of soil for every 4 flower beds. How many bags for 20 flower beds?

1.10 Converting Measurement Units

Learning Goals

- Use ratio reasoning to convert between measurement units
- Convert within the same system (inches to feet, grams to kilograms)
- Track units to avoid mistakes

Unit Conversion Is a Ratio

Converting units is just using a ratio. Every conversion is a rate:

- 1 foot $= 12$ inches $\rightarrow$ ratio of $1:12$
- 1 meter $= 100$ centimeters $\rightarrow$ ratio of $1:100$
- 1 hour $= 60$ minutes $\rightarrow$ ratio of $1:60$

Bigger unit $\rightarrow$ smaller unit: multiply.

Smaller unit $\rightarrow$ bigger unit: divide.

Convert Using Ratios

Bigger to Smaller:

Convert 3.5 hours to minutes.

1 hour $= 60$ minutes. Bigger $\rightarrow$ smaller means multiply: $3.5 \times 60 = 210$.

Answer: 3.5 **hours** $=$ 210 **minutes**

Smaller to Bigger:

Convert 450 centimeters to meters.

1 meter $= 100$ cm. Smaller $\rightarrow$ bigger means divide: $450 \div 100 = 4.5$.

Answer: 450 **cm** $=$ 4.5 **m**

"Multiply to go small, divide to go big. The number gets bigger when the unit gets smaller!"

Unit Conversion Practice

Convert

1. 5 feet = ________ inches
2. 240 minutes = ________ hours
3. 3 kilometers = ________ meters
4. 2,500 grams = ________ kilograms

Word Problems

5. A movie is 135 minutes long. How many hours and minutes is that?
6. A ribbon is 2.5 yards long. How many inches is that? (1 yard = 36 inches)

★ 1.11 Personal Financial Literacy ★

Learning Goals

- Distinguish between needs and wants
- Compare income sources and payment methods
- Understand credit, debit, and the value of saving

Needs vs. Wants

Needs are things you must have to survive: food, shelter, clothing, healthcare.

Wants are things you would like but can live without: video games, designer clothes, concert tickets.

A smart budget covers needs first, then uses leftover money for wants and savings.

Ways to Pay

- **Cash / Debit card** — money you already have. No extra cost.
- **Credit card** — borrowed money. If you don't pay the full bill, you are charged **interest**.
- **Check** — written order to your bank to pay someone from your account.

Credit is convenient, but interest adds up fast. Always try to pay the full balance each month!

Saving vs. Spending

Maria earns $\$40$ per week babysitting. She saves 25% and spends the rest.

Solution:

1. Savings per week: $0.25 \times \$40 = \$10$.
2. Spending per week: $\$40 - \$10 = \$30$.
3. After 8 weeks: $8 \times \$10 = \$80$ saved.

Answer: After 8 weeks Maria has saved $\$80$.

> *The "pay yourself first" rule: put money into savings **before** you spend on wants!*

Financial Literacy Practice

Needs and Wants

1. Classify each item as a need or a want: (a) rent, (b) new sneakers, (c) groceries, (d) streaming service.

Income and Saving

2. Jake mows lawns and earns $\$60$ per week. He saves 20% and spends the rest. How much does he save each week?

3. After 10 weeks of saving, Jake wants to buy a bike for $\$100$. Can he afford it?

Credit and Interest

4. A credit card charges 15% annual interest. You owe $\$200$ and don't pay it for 1 year. How much interest is added?

5. Why might someone choose a debit card over a credit card?

1.12 Proportional vs. Non-Proportional Relationships

Learning Goals

- Identify proportional relationships in tables and graphs
- Recognize non-proportional relationships
- Find the constant of proportionality

Proportional Relationships

A relationship is **proportional** if:

- The ratio $\frac{y}{x}$ is the **same** for every pair.
- The graph is a **straight line through the origin** $(0, 0)$.
- The equation has the form $y = kx$, where k is the **constant of proportionality**.

x	y	$y \div x$
2	6	3
4	12	3
5	15	3

Every ratio is 3, so $y = 3x$. This is proportional with $k = 3$.

Proportional or Not?

Table A:

x	1	2	3
y	5	7	9

Ratios: $5/1 = 5$, $7/2 = 3.5$, $9/3 = 3$. Not constant $\rightarrow$

Answer: Non-proportional.

Table B:

x	2	4	6
y	8	16	24

Ratios: $8/2 = 4$, $16/4 = 4$, $24/6 = 4$. Constant $\rightarrow$

Answer: Proportional, $k = 4$.

TIP

If you see a y-intercept that is NOT zero (like $y = 2x + 3$), the relationship is **non-proportional**.

Proportional vs. Non-Proportional Practice

Classify

1. $y = 7x$. Proportional or non-proportional?
2. $y = 3x + 1$. Proportional or non-proportional?
3. A table shows $(1, 4)$, $(2, 8)$, $(3, 12)$. Is it proportional? If so, find k.

Real-World

4. A taxi charges \$3 base fee plus \$2 per mile. Is cost proportional to distance?
5. Bananas cost \$0.60 per pound with no other fees. Is cost proportional to weight? Find k.

★ 1.13 Financial Literacy: Budgeting and Saving ★

Learning Goals

- Create and analyze a simple budget with fixed and variable expenses
- Compare savings plans using simple interest
- Understand opportunity cost when making financial decisions

Building a Budget

A **budget** is a plan for how to spend and save money.

- **Income** — money you earn (allowance, jobs, gifts).
- **Fixed expenses** — costs that stay the same each month (rent, subscriptions).
- **Variable expenses** — costs that change (food, entertainment, gas).
- **Savings** — money set aside for the future.

Income $-$ **Expenses** $-$ **Savings** $= 0$. **Every dollar should have a job!**

Ana's Monthly Budget

Ana earns $\$300$/month. Her expenses: phone $\$30$ (fixed), lunch $\$50$ (variable), entertainment $\$40$ (variable). She saves the rest.

Solution:

1. Total expenses: $\$30 + \$50 + \$40 = \$120$.

2. Savings: $\$300 - \$120 = \$180$.
3. Savings rate: $\$180/\$300 = 60\%$.

Answer: Ana saves $\$180$ per month (60% of income).

Opportunity Cost

Every choice has a trade-off. The **opportunity cost** is what you give up when you choose one option over another.

Example: You have $\$50$. You buy a video game instead of saving. The opportunity cost is the interest you would have earned on that $\$50$.

"A good rule of thumb: save at least 20% of your income. Pay needs first, save second, then spend on wants!"

Budgeting Practice

Build a Budget

1. Diego earns $200/month. His expenses: bus pass $25, food $60, clothes $35. How much can he save?

2. What percent of Diego's income goes to savings?

Compare Savings Plans

3. Plan A: Save $100 at 3% simple interest for 2 years. Plan B: Save $100 at 5% for 1 year. Which earns more interest?

Opportunity Cost

4. You can spend $75 on shoes or save it at 4% for 3 years. What is the opportunity cost of buying the shoes?

5. Maya can work 5 extra hours at $10/hour or go to a concert. What is the opportunity cost of the concert?

CHAPTER

2

The Number System

What's Inside

2.1 Dividing Fractions by Fractions

Dividing Fractions by Fractions

Learning Goals

- Understand what it means to divide a fraction by a fraction
- Use the "Keep–Change–Flip" method to divide fractions
- Connect fraction division to real-world situations
- Check your answers using multiplication

When Do You Divide Fractions?

You have $\frac{3}{4}$ of a pizza left. You want to split it equally among friends so each person gets $\frac{1}{4}$ of the whole pizza. How many people can you feed?

That's $\frac{3}{4} \div \frac{1}{4}$ — and the answer is 3 people. You just divided a fraction by a fraction!

What Does Fraction Division Mean?

When you divide by a fraction, you're asking: **"How many of this fraction fit into that amount?"**

$\frac{3}{4} \div \frac{1}{4}$ means: "How many $\frac{1}{4}$'s are in $\frac{3}{4}$?"

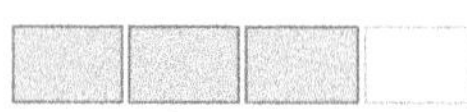

You can count: there are 3 pieces of size $\frac{1}{4}$ in $\frac{3}{4}$. So $\frac{3}{4} \div \frac{1}{4} = 3$.

Keep–Change–Flip (Dividing Fractions)

1. **Keep** the first fraction exactly as it is.
2. **Change** the division sign (÷) to multiplication (×).
3. **Flip** the second fraction (swap the numerator and denominator). This flipped fraction is called the **reciprocal**.
4. Multiply straight across: numerators together, denominators together.
5. Simplify if possible.

> *The **reciprocal** of $\frac{2}{3}$ is $\frac{3}{2}$. Just flip it! Every fraction has a reciprocal — except 0.*

Divide $\frac{2}{3} \div \frac{4}{5}$

Solution:

1. **Keep** the first fraction: $\frac{2}{3}$
2. **Change** ÷ to ×
3. **Flip** $\frac{4}{5}$ to get $\frac{5}{4}$
4. Multiply: $\frac{2}{3} \times \frac{5}{4} = \frac{2 \times 5}{3 \times 4} = \frac{10}{12}$
5. Simplify: $\frac{10}{12} = \frac{5}{6}$

Answer: $\frac{2}{3} \div \frac{4}{5} = \frac{5}{6}$

TIP

To check your answer, multiply it by the divisor. If you get back the dividend, you're correct!

$\frac{5}{6} \times \frac{4}{5} = \frac{20}{30} = \frac{2}{3}$ ✓

A Real-World Problem

A ribbon is $\frac{7}{8}$ of a yard long. You need pieces that are each $\frac{1}{4}$ of a yard. How many pieces can you cut?

Solution:

1. Write the division: $\frac{7}{8} \div \frac{1}{4}$
2. Keep–Change–Flip: $\frac{7}{8} \times \frac{4}{1}$
3. Multiply: $\frac{7 \times 4}{8 \times 1} = \frac{28}{8}$
4. Simplify: $\frac{28}{8} = \frac{7}{2} = 3\frac{1}{2}$

Answer: You can cut 3 full pieces (with some ribbon left over).

Spot the Error

What Went Wrong? Maya solved $\frac{3}{5} \div \frac{2}{7}$ like this:

"I'll flip the *first* fraction: $\frac{5}{3} \times \frac{2}{7} = \frac{10}{21}$"

What did Maya do wrong? ____________________

The correct answer is: __________

Maya flipped the wrong fraction! You always flip the ***second*** *fraction (the one you're dividing by). The correct work is:*

$\frac{3}{5} \times \frac{7}{2} = \frac{21}{10} = 2\frac{1}{10}$

Dividing a Whole Number by a Fraction

How many $\frac{1}{3}$-cup servings are in 4 cups of soup?

Solution:

1. Write 4 as a fraction: $\frac{4}{1}$
2. Set up: $\frac{4}{1} \div \frac{1}{3}$
3. Keep–Change–Flip: $\frac{4}{1} \times \frac{3}{1} = \frac{12}{1} = 12$

Answer: There are 12 servings.

Remember!

- Dividing by a fraction less than 1 gives you a **bigger** answer.
- Dividing by a fraction greater than 1 gives you a **smaller** answer.
- Always simplify your final answer.
- Check by multiplying: answer $\times$ divisor $=$ dividend.

Dividing Fractions — Practice

Divide and Simplify

1. $\frac{1}{2} \div \frac{1}{4} =$ ________

2. $\frac{3}{5} \div \frac{1}{2} =$ ________

3. $\frac{5}{6} \div \frac{2}{3} =$ ________

4. $\frac{4}{9} \div \frac{2}{3} =$ ________

Whole Numbers and Fractions

5. $3 \div \frac{1}{5} =$ ________

6. $\frac{7}{8} \div 2 =$ ________

Word Problems

7. A trail mix recipe needs $\frac{3}{4}$ cup of raisins. Each scoop holds $\frac{1}{8}$ cup. How many scoops do you need?

8. A board is $\frac{5}{6}$ of a foot long. You cut it into pieces that are each $\frac{1}{3}$ of a foot. How many pieces do you get?

Challenge!

1. You have $\frac{2}{3}$ of a gallon of paint. Each wall needs $\frac{1}{6}$ of a gallon. How many walls can you paint? If a room has 4 walls, do you have enough paint for the whole room?

2.2 Multi-Digit Division

Multi-Digit Division

Learning Goals

- Divide multi-digit whole numbers using the standard algorithm
- Estimate quotients before dividing
- Check answers using multiplication

I can divide by one-digit numbers, but what about dividing by bigger numbers like 24 or 36?

Same idea — just more steps! Let's walk through it.

Long Division Steps

1. **Divide** — How many times does the divisor go into the current digits?
2. **Multiply** — Divisor $\times$ your quotient digit.
3. **Subtract** — Subtract the product from the current number.

4. **Bring down** — Bring down the next digit.
5. **Repeat** until there are no more digits to bring down.

> *Remember the phrase: **"Does McDonald's Sell Burgers Raw?"** — Divide, Multiply, Subtract, Bring down, Repeat!*

Divide $846 \div 18$

Step by Step:

1. **Estimate first:** $846 \div 18 \approx 800 \div 20 = 40$. So the answer should be close to 40.
2. **Divide:** 18 goes into 84 how many times? $18 \times 4 = 72$ and $18 \times 5 = 90$ (too big). Write 4 above the 4 in 846.
3. **Multiply:** $4 \times 18 = 72$
4. **Subtract:** $84 - 72 = 12$
5. **Bring down** the 6: now you have 126.
6. **Divide:** 18 goes into 126 how many times? $18 \times 7 = 126$. Write 7.
7. **Multiply:** $7 \times 18 = 126$
8. **Subtract:** $126 - 126 = 0$. No remainder!

Answer: $846 \div 18 = 47$

Check: $47 \times 18 = 846$ ✓

Why Estimate First?

Estimating before you divide helps you:

- Know roughly what to expect (so you catch big mistakes).
- Choose better quotient digits during long division.
- Build strong number sense.

Quick estimation trick: Round both numbers to "friendly" numbers, then divide.

$$4{,}356 \div 52 \approx 4{,}000 \div 50 = 80$$

Division with a Remainder

Divide $1{,}537 \div 24$.

Solution:

1. **Estimate:** $1{,}537 \div 24 \approx 1{,}500 \div 25 = 60$
2. 24 into 15? Doesn't go. Try 153: $24 \times 6 = 144$. Write 6.
3. Subtract: $153 - 144 = 9$. Bring down 7: now 97.
4. 24 into 97: $24 \times 4 = 96$. Write 4.
5. Subtract: $97 - 96 = 1$. No more digits to bring down.

Answer: $1{,}537 \div 24 = 64$ **R** 1

Check: $64 \times 24 + 1 = 1{,}536 + 1 = 1{,}537$ ✓

TIP

Always check: quotient × divisor + remainder = dividend. If it doesn't match, go back and find your mistake!

Remember!

- The remainder must always be **less than** the divisor.
- If your remainder is bigger than the divisor, your quotient digit is too small — try a larger one.
- Line up your digits carefully. Sloppy columns cause errors!

Multi-Digit Division — Practice

Divide Using the Standard Algorithm

1. $756 \div 12 =$ ________
2. $972 \div 27 =$ ________
3. $1{,}248 \div 16 =$ ________
4. $2{,}340 \div 45 =$ ________

Division with Remainders

5. $895 \div 14 =$ ________
6. $3{,}217 \div 38 =$ ________

Word Problems

7. A school is ordering buses for a field trip. There are 342 students and each bus holds 36 passengers. How many buses are needed?

8. A factory makes 2,856 toy cars in 14 hours. How many cars does it make per hour?

Challenge!

1. Without doing the full division, explain how you know that $4{,}753 \div 23$ has a two-digit quotient (not three digits). Then find the actual answer.

★ 2.3 Decimal Operations ★

Decimal Operations

Learning Goals

- Add, subtract, multiply, and divide decimals fluently
- Use place value to line up decimals correctly
- Estimate to check if answers are reasonable

Decimal operations follow the same rules as whole-number operations — you just need to keep track of the decimal point!

Adding and Subtracting Decimals

The key rule: **line up the decimal points**, then add or subtract as usual.

$$\begin{array}{r} 12.350 \\ +\ 4.075 \\ \hline 16.425 \end{array} \qquad \begin{array}{r} 8.200 \\ -\ 3.146 \\ \hline 5.054 \end{array}$$

TIP

Fill in trailing zeros so both numbers have the same number of decimal places. It makes subtraction much easier! 8.2 becomes 8.200.

Multiplying Decimals

Multiply as if the numbers were whole numbers. Then count the **total decimal places** in both factors and place the decimal point in the product.

$$2.4 \times 0.13 = ?$$

1. Ignore the decimals: $24 \times 13 = 312$
2. Count decimal places: 2.4 has 1 place, 0.13 has 2 places $\rightarrow$ total 3 places
3. Place the decimal: $312 \rightarrow 0.312$

Answer: $2.4 \times 0.13 = 0.312$

Quick check: 2.4×0.13 should be less than 2.4 (because you're multiplying by something less than 1). Is $0.312 < 2.4$? Yes! Makes sense.

Dividing Decimals

To divide by a decimal, **move the decimal point** in the divisor to make it a whole number. Move the decimal in the dividend the same number of places.

$$7.56 \div 0.3$$

1. Move the decimal in 0.3 one place right: $0.3 \rightarrow 3$

2. Move the decimal in 7.56 one place right: $7.56 \to 75.6$
3. Now divide: $75.6 \div 3 = 25.2$

Answer: $7.56 \div 0.3 = 25.2$

Putting It All Together

A phone plan costs $\$34.50$ per month. If you also pay a one-time setup fee of $\$12.75$, what is the total cost for 6 months?

Solution:

1. Monthly cost for 6 months: $34.50 \times 6 = 207.00$
2. Add the setup fee: $207.00 + 12.75 = 219.75$

Answer: The total cost is $\$219.75$.

Spot the Error

A student computed 3.5×2.4 and got 84.0.

What went wrong? The student forgot to place the decimal point. $35 \times 24 = 840$, but there are 2 total decimal places $(1 + 1)$, so the answer should be 8.40 (or 8.4).

Estimate check: $3.5 \times 2.4 \approx 4 \times 2 = 8$. The answer 84 is way too big!

Remember!

- **Add/Subtract:** Line up the decimal points.
- **Multiply:** Count total decimal places in both factors.
- **Divide:** Move the decimal to make the divisor a whole number.
- **Always:** Estimate first to check if your answer is reasonable.

Decimal Operations — Practice

Add and Subtract

1. $14.63 + 7.089 =$ ________
2. $50.2 - 13.85 =$ ________
3. $100 - 27.456 =$ ________
4. $3.007 + 12.93 =$ ________

Multiply

5. $6.3 \times 4.1 =$ ________
6. $0.07 \times 0.5 =$ ________

Divide

7. $9.12 \div 0.4 =$ ________
8. $15.6 \div 1.2 =$ ________

Word Problems

9. You buy 3 notebooks at \$2.49 each and a pen for \$1.75. What is the total cost?

10. A relay team of 4 runners finished a race in 52.8 seconds total. If each runner ran the same time, how long did each runner take?

Challenge!

1. Without a calculator, find 0.012×0.05 and explain how you placed the decimal point.

★ 2.4 Greatest Common Factor and Least Common Multiple ★

Greatest Common Factor and Least Common Multiple

Learning Goals

- Find the greatest common factor (GCF) of two numbers up to 100
- Find the least common multiple (LCM) of two numbers up to 12
- Use factor lists and prime factorization

Vocabulary

Factor — A number that divides evenly into another number. The factors of 12 are $1, 2, 3, 4, 6, 12$.

Multiple — The result of multiplying a number by a whole number. Multiples of 4: $4, 8, 12, 16, 20, \dots$

GCF — The **greatest common factor** — the largest factor shared by two numbers.

LCM — The **least common multiple** — the smallest multiple shared by two numbers (other than 0).

Finding the GCF

To find the GCF of two numbers, list all the factors of each number and pick the **largest one they share**.

Find the GCF of 24 and 36:

- Factors of 24: $1, 2, 3, 4, 6, 8, 12, 24$

- Factors of 36: $1, 2, 3, 4, 6, 9, 12, 18, 36$
- Common factors: $1, 2, 3, 4, 6, 12$

Answer: GCF of 24 and 36 is 12.

GCF Using Prime Factorization

Find the GCF of 48 and 60.

Prime factorizations:

- $48 = 2 \times 2 \times 2 \times 2 \times 3$
- $60 = 2 \times 2 \times 3 \times 5$

Circle the prime factors they **share**:

- Shared: $2 \times 2 \times 3 = 12$

Multiply the shared primes together to get the GCF.

Answer: GCF$(48, 60) \quad = \quad 12$

“Think of the GCF as the biggest “building block” that fits evenly into both numbers. It's super useful for simplifying fractions!”

Finding the LCM

To find the LCM, list multiples of each number until you find the **smallest one they share**.

Find the LCM of 6 and 8:

- Multiples of 6: $6, 12, 18, \mathbf{24}, 30, \ldots$
- Multiples of 8: $8, 16, \mathbf{24}, 32, \ldots$

Answer: LCM of 6 and 8 is 24.

LCM Using Prime Factorization

Find the LCM of 9 and 12.

Solution:

1. Prime factorizations: $9 = 3 \times 3$ and $12 = 2 \times 2 \times 3$
2. Take the **highest power** of each prime: 2^2 and 3^2
3. Multiply: $2^2 \times 3^2 = 4 \times 9 = 36$

Answer: LCM$(9, 12) = 36$

GCF vs. LCM	When to Use Each

GCF is for **splitting things into equal groups**:
- Simplifying fractions
- Dividing items into equal groups
- "What's the most you can split evenly?"

LCM is for **finding when things line up**:
- Adding fractions (common denominator)
- Repeating schedules
- "When will they happen at the same time?"

A Real-World GCF Problem

You have 18 apples and 24 granola bars. You want to make gift bags with the same number of apples and the same number of granola bars in each bag, with nothing left over. What is the greatest number of bags you can make?

Solution:

1. Find GCF$(18, 24)$: factors of 18 are $1, 2, 3, 6, 9, 18$; factors of 24 are $1, 2, 3, 4, 6, 8, 12, 24$.
2. GCF $= 6$, so you can make 6 bags.
3. Each bag gets $18 \div 6 = 3$ apples and $24 \div 6 = 4$ granola bars.

Answer: 6 **bags (**3 **apples and** 4 **granola bars each).**

A Real-World LCM Problem

Hot dogs come in packs of 8. Buns come in packs of 6. What is the least number of each you should buy so you have the same number of hot dogs and buns?

Solution:

1. Find LCM$(8, 6)$: multiples of 8 are $8, 16, 24, \ldots$; multiples of 6 are $6, 12, 18, 24, \ldots$
2. LCM $= 24$
3. You need $24 \div 8 = 3$ packs of hot dogs and $24 \div 6 = 4$ packs of buns.

Answer: Buy 3 **packs of hot dogs and** 4 **packs of buns (**24 **of each).**

GCF and LCM — Practice

Find the GCF

1. GCF of 16 and 40: __________
2. GCF of 36 and 54: __________
3. GCF of 28 and 42: __________
4. GCF of 100 and 75: __________

Find the LCM

5. LCM of 4 and 10: __________
6. LCM of 6 and 9: __________
7. LCM of 8 and 12: __________
8. LCM of 5 and 7: __________

Word Problems

9. You have 30 pencils and 48 erasers. You want to put them into identical goodie bags with no items left over. What is the greatest number of bags you can make?

10. Two buses leave the station at the same time. Bus A returns every 12 minutes. Bus B returns every 8 minutes. In how many minutes will they both be at the station again at the same time?

Challenge!

1.

2. The GCF of any number and itself is always that number. True ◯ False ◯

3.

4. The LCM of two numbers is always bigger than both numbers. **True** ◯ **False** ◯

2.5 The Distributive Property with Common Factors

Learning Goals

- Rewrite a sum using the distributive property
- Factor out the GCF from two numbers
- Use the distributive property for mental math

The Distributive Property

The **distributive property** says:

$$a(b + c) = a \times b + a \times c$$

You can also go backwards. If two numbers share a common factor, pull it out:

$$36 + 8 = 4(9 + 2)$$

Both 36 and 8 are divisible by 4. So factor out the 4.

Factor a Sum

Rewrite $24 + 18$ using the distributive property.

Solution:

1. Find the GCF of 24 and 18. GCF $= 6$.

2. Divide each number by 6: $24 \div 6 = 4$ and $18 \div 6 = 3$.
3. Write: $24 + 18 = 6(4 + 3)$.

Answer: $24 + 18 = 6(4 + 3) = 6 \times 7 = 42$

"Think of the distributive property like un-dealing cards. If every group got the same base amount, you can write it once on the outside!"

Spot the Error

Mia wrote: $20 + 15 = 5(4 + 5)$.

What went wrong? $15 \div 5 = 3$, not 5. The correct answer is $5(4 + 3)$.

Distributive Property Practice

Rewrite Using the Distributive Property

1. $16 + 28 =$ ______________
2. $45 + 30 =$ ______________
3. $21 + 35 =$ ______________
4. $54 + 36 =$ ______________

Mental Math

5. Use the distributive property to find 6×53 in your head.
6. A store sells shirts for $\$12$ each. You buy 8 shirts. Use the distributive property to find the total.

2.6 Understanding Positive and Negative Numbers

Learning Goals

- Understand that positive and negative numbers show opposite directions
- Use positive and negative numbers in real-life contexts
- Begin adding integers using a number line

Positive, Negative, and Zero

Numbers go in **two directions** from zero:

- **Positive numbers** (+) are greater than zero: $1, 2, 3, \ldots$
- **Negative numbers** (−) are less than zero: $-1, -2, -3, \ldots$
- **Zero** is neither positive nor negative.

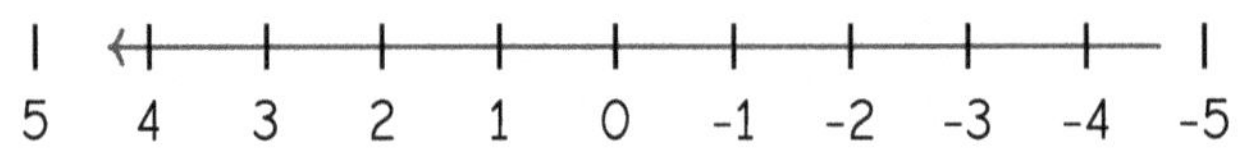

Negative numbers are to the **left** of zero. Positive numbers are to the **right**.

Where Do You See Negative Numbers?

- **Temperature:** $-10°$F means 10 degrees below zero.
- **Money:** $-\$25$ means you owe $\$25$.
- **Elevation:** -50 feet means 50 feet below sea level.

In each case, **zero is the starting point**: $0°$, no debt, sea level.

Adding Integers — A Preview

You can add integers by moving on the number line:

- Adding a **positive** number $\rightarrow$ move **right**.
- Adding a **negative** number $\rightarrow$ move **left**.

Example: $3+(-5)$. Start at 3, move 5 left $\rightarrow$ land on -2.

Quick rules:

- **Same signs:** Add the numbers, keep the sign. $(-4)+(-3)=-7$.
- **Different signs:** Subtract, keep the sign of the bigger number. $(-4)+7=3$.

> *Zero is not "nothing" — it is the **boundary** between positive and negative!*

Positive and Negative Numbers Practice

Write the Number

1. A submarine is 200 feet below sea level. Write this as an integer.
2. The temperature dropped 8 degrees below zero. Write the temperature.

Adding Integers

3. $5 + (-3) =$ ________
4. $(-6) + (-4) =$ ________
5. $(-7) + 10 =$ ________

Real-Life Context

6. You have $15 in your account and spend $20. Write an addition equation and find your balance.

★ 2.7 Opposites and Absolute Value ★

Learning Goals

- Find the opposite of any number
- Understand that absolute value is distance from zero
- Apply absolute value to financial and real-world contexts

Opposites

Two numbers are **opposites** if they are the same distance from zero but on different sides.

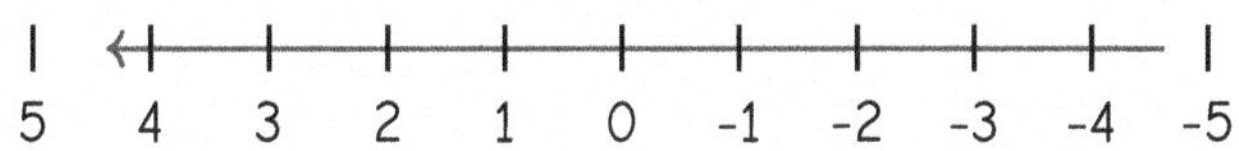

- The opposite of 4 is -4.
- The opposite of -3 is 3.
- The opposite of 0 is 0.

A number plus its opposite always equals zero: $5+(-5)=0$.

Absolute Value

The **absolute value** of a number is its distance from zero. Distance is always positive (or zero).

We write absolute value with bars: $|-7|=7$ and $|7|=7$.

Both -7 and 7 are 7 units from zero.

Absolute value strips away the sign. It only tells you "how far," not "which direction."

Absolute Value and Money

Who owes more?

Riley's account shows $-\$35$. Jordan's shows $-\$20$. Who is farther from a zero balance?

Compare distances from $\$0$: $|-35| = 35$ and $|-20| = 20$.

Since $35 > 20$, Riley is farther from zero.

Answer: Riley owes more.

Profit or Loss?

A business had $-\$500$ in January and $+\$300$ in February. Which month had a bigger change from break-even ($\$0$)?

$|-500| = 500$ and $|300| = 300$.

Answer: January had a bigger change ($\$500$).

> *"Think of absolute value as "How many dollars from zero?" It does not matter if you gained or lost — just the size of the change."*

Opposites and Absolute Value Practice

Find the Opposite and Absolute Value

1. Opposite of 9

2. Opposite of -12

3. $|-15| =$

4. $|8| =$

Financial Applications

5. Account A: $-\$45$. Account B: $-\$30$. Which account is farther from zero?

6. A store had a loss of $-\$200$ in May and a profit of $+\$150$ in June. Which month had a larger change from break-even?

7. $|-6| > |5|$ True ◯ False ◯

2.8 Rational Numbers on the Number Line

Learning Goals

- Place integers, fractions, and decimals on a number line
- Explain placement using distance and direction from 0
- Understand that rational numbers include all of these forms

A rational number is any number that can be written as a fraction $\frac{a}{b}$ where $b \neq 0$. This includes integers, fractions, and decimals.

Placing Numbers on the Number Line

Every rational number has an exact spot on the number line.

Steps:

1. Decide the sign: positive (right of 0) or negative (left of 0).
2. Find the whole number part to know which two integers it falls between.
3. Use the fraction or decimal part to find the exact spot.

-1.5 **is halfway between** -2 **and** -1**. It is** 1.5 **units to the left of** 0.

Plot $-\frac{3}{4}$ on a Number Line

Solution:

1. Negative → left of zero.
2. $\frac{3}{4}$ is between 0 and 1, so $-\frac{3}{4}$ is between -1 and 0.
3. Divide the space from -1 to 0 into 4 equal parts. Go 3 parts from 0.

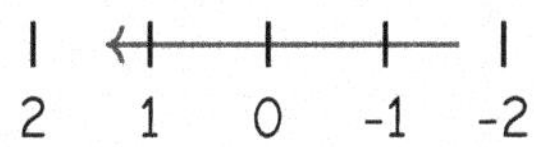

$-\frac{3}{4}$ is $\frac{3}{4}$ of a unit to the left of zero.

TIP

Convert fractions to decimals if it helps: $-\frac{3}{4} = -0.75$. Then place it on the number line.

Number Line Practice

Place on a Number Line

1. Where does $\frac{1}{2}$ go on a number line? Between which two integers?
2. Where does -2.25 go? Between which two integers?
3. Place $-\frac{5}{3}$ on a number line. Between which two integers?

Order and Compare

4. Which is farther from 0: -3.5 or 2.8?
5. List these in order from least to greatest: $\frac{1}{4}$, -1, 0.75, $-\frac{1}{2}$
6. -0.5 and $-\frac{1}{2}$ are the same point on the number line. True ◯ False ◯

2.9 The Coordinate Plane

Learning Goals

- Plot points with positive and negative coordinates
- Identify the four quadrants
- Describe how changing signs reflects points across axes

The Four Quadrants

A coordinate plane has two axes that cross at the **origin** $(0, 0)$. They divide the plane into four quadrants:

Quadrant	Signs of (x, y)	Example
I	$(+, +)$	$(3, 4)$
II	$(-, +)$	$(-2, 5)$
III	$(-, -)$	$(-1, -3)$
IV	$(+, -)$	$(4, -2)$

The first number (x) tells left/right. The second number (y) tells up/down.

Plot and Reflect

Plot $A = (3, 2)$. Then plot its reflection across the y-axis.

Solution:

1. Start at the origin. Move 3 right and 2 up. That is $A = (3, 2)$.
2. To reflect across the y-axis, flip the x-coordinate sign.
3. The reflection is $(-3, 2)$.

Answer: The reflection of $(3, 2)$ across the y-axis is $(-3, 2)$.

“Reflecting across the y-axis changes the sign of x. Reflecting across the x-axis changes the sign of y. The other coordinate stays the same!”

Coordinate Plane Practice

Name the Quadrant

1. $(5, -3)$ is in Quadrant _____

2. $(-4, 7)$ is in Quadrant _____

Reflections

3. What is the reflection of $(2, -5)$ across the x-axis?

4. What is the reflection of $(-6, 1)$ across the y-axis?

Think Deeper

5. A point starts at $(-3, 4)$. It is reflected across the x-axis, then across the y-axis. Where does it end up?

6. The point $(0, -4)$ is on the y-axis. True ◯ False ◯

2.10 Comparing and Ordering Rational Numbers

Learning Goals

- Compare rational numbers using $<$, $>$, and $=$
- Order rational numbers from least to greatest
- Explain comparisons in real-world contexts

Comparing on the Number Line

On a number line, numbers get **larger** as you move right.

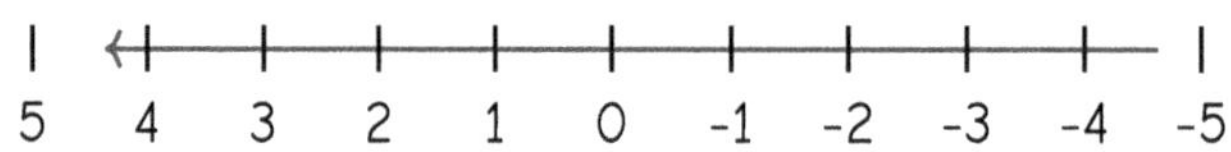

- -3 is to the left of 1, so $-3 < 1$.
- -1 is to the right of -4, so $-1 > -4$.

With negative numbers, the one closer to zero is greater. $-2 > -7$ because -2 is closer to zero.

Order a Mixed Set

Order from least to greatest: $-1.5,\ \frac{3}{4},\ \ -3,\ \ 0,\ \ 2.1$

Solution:

1. Convert to decimals for easy comparison: $-1.5, 0.75, -3, 0, 2.1$.

2. Plot mentally on a number line, left to right.

3. Order: $-3 < -1.5 < 0 < 0.75 < 2.1$.

Answer: $-3, \quad -1.5, \quad 0, \quad \frac{3}{4}, \quad 2.1$

TIP

Don't confuse number order with absolute value! $-8 < 3$ as a number, but $|-8| = 8 > |3| = 3$ in absolute value.

"When comparing negatives, think about a thermometer. $-5°$ is colder (smaller) than $-2°$ even though 5 looks bigger!"

Comparing and Ordering Practice

Compare: Write $<$, $>$, or $=$

1. -7 _____ -3

2. 0 _____ -6

3. -2.5 _____ -2.5

4. $\frac{1}{3}$ _____ $-\frac{1}{2}$

Order and Explain

5. Order from least to greatest: $5, -8, 3, -1, 0$

6. The temperature on Monday was $-4°C$. On Tuesday it was $-9°C$. Which day was colder?

2.11 Distance on the Coordinate Plane

Learning Goals

- Find horizontal and vertical distances between points
- Use absolute value to compute distance
- Apply distance to real-world grid problems

Distance = Absolute Value of the Difference

When two points share the same x or the same y, you can find the distance between them:

Same x (vertical distance): Subtract the y-values and take the absolute value.

$$\text{Distance} = |y_1 - y_2|$$

Same y (horizontal distance): Subtract the x-values and take the absolute value.

$$\text{Distance} = |x_1 - x_2|$$

Absolute value makes sure the distance is always positive — you can't walk a negative number of steps!

Find the Distance

Vertical:

Find the distance between $(3, -2)$ and $(3, 5)$.

Both have $x = 3$. Subtract y-values: $|-2 - 5| = |-7| = 7$ units.

Horizontal:

Find the distance between $(-4, 1)$ and $(2, 1)$.

Both have $y = 1$. Subtract x-values: $|-4 - 2| = |-6| = 6$ units.

Distance Practice

Find the Distance

1. Distance between $(1, 4)$ and $(1, -3)$
2. Distance between $(-5, 2)$ and $(3, 2)$
3. Distance between $(0, -6)$ and $(0, 4)$
4. Distance between $(-3, -1)$ and $(-3, -9)$

Word Problems

5. A map grid shows a school at $(2, 5)$ and a library at $(2, -3)$. Each unit is 1 block. How many blocks apart are they?
6. Two traffic lights are at $(-7, 4)$ and $(5, 4)$. How far apart are they?

2.12 Integer Addition and Subtraction

Learning Goals

- Add integers using number line models and sign rules
- Subtract integers by adding the opposite
- Solve real-world problems with integer addition and subtraction

Adding Integers

Same signs: Add the numbers and keep the sign.

$(-3) + (-5) = -8$ $4 + 7 = 11$

Different signs: Subtract the smaller absolute value from the larger. Keep the sign of the number with the greater absolute value.

$(-8) + 3 = -5$ $(-4) + 9 = 5$

Think of positives as gains and negatives as losses. Combine them!

Subtracting Integers

To subtract an integer, **add its opposite**:

$a - b = a + (-b)$

Examples:

- $7 - 10 = 7 + (-10) = -3$

- $(-3)-(-5)=(-3)+5=2$

"Subtracting a negative is like adding a positive." Two negatives make a positive!

Temperature Change

At midnight the temperature was $-4°$F. By noon it rose 15 degrees. What was the noon temperature?

$-4+15=11.$

Answer: $11°$F

Stuck? Use a number line! Start at the first number. Move right for positive, left for negative.

Integer Addition and Subtraction Practice

Compute

1. $(-6) + (-8) =$ __________
2. $(-12) + 7 =$ __________
3. $9 - 15 =$ __________
4. $(-3) - (-10) =$ __________

Word Problems

5. A diver at -20 feet descends another 15 feet. What is the new depth?
6. A football team gains 8 yards, then loses 12 yards. What is the net yardage?

2.13 Integer Multiplication and Division

Learning Goals

- Multiply integers using sign rules
- Divide integers using sign rules
- Apply integer operations to real-world problems

Sign Rules for Multiplication and Division

The rules are the same for both operations:

Signs	Result
Positive × Positive	Positive
Negative × Negative	Positive
Positive × Negative	Negative
Negative × Positive	Negative

Same signs → positive result. Different signs → negative result.

Applying the Sign Rules

Multiply:

$(-6) \times 4 = ?$

Different signs → negative. $6 \times 4 = 24$.

Answer: -24

Divide:

$(-36) \div (-9) = ?$

Same signs → positive. $36 \div 9 = 4$.

Answer: 4

Multi-step:

$(-2) \times (-3) \times (-4) = ?$

First: $(-2) \times (-3) = 6$. Then: $6 \times (-4) = -24$.

Answer: -24

> *Count the negatives! An **even** number of negatives gives a positive. An **odd** number gives a negative.*

Integer Multiply and Divide Practice

Compute

1. $(-7) \times 5 =$ __________

2. $(-8) \times (-3) =$ __________

3. $(-48) \div 6 =$ __________

4. $(-56) \div (-7) =$ __________

Word Problems

5. A stock lost $3 per day for 5 days. What was the total change?

6. The temperature dropped 24°F over 6 hours at a steady rate. How much did it change each hour?

CHAPTER

3

Expressions and Equations

What's Inside

3.1 Exponents and Order of Operations

Learning Goals

- Write repeated multiplication using exponents
- Evaluate expressions with whole-number exponents
- Apply the order of operations (PEMDAS)

Exponents

An **exponent** tells you how many times to multiply the base by itself.

$3^4 = 3 \times 3 \times 3 \times 3 = 81$

- 3 is the **base** — the number being multiplied.
- 4 is the **exponent** — how many times.
- We say "3 to the fourth power."

Any number to the power of 1 is itself: $7^1 = 7$. Any number to the power of 0 is 1: $5^0 = 1$.

Order of Operations (PEMDAS)

Evaluate: $5 + 2 \times 3^2$

Solution:

1. **E**xponents first: $3^2 = 9$.

2. Multiply: $2 \times 9 = 18$.
3. Add: $5 + 18 = 23$.

Answer: 23

*PEMDAS: **P**arentheses, **E**xponents, **M**ultiply/**D**ivide (left to right), **A**dd/**S**ubtract (left to right).*

Exponents and Order of Operations Practice

Write Using Exponents

1. $7 \times 7 \times 7$

2. $2 \times 2 \times 2 \times 2 \times 2$

Evaluate

3. 4^3

4. $10^2 - 6 \times 5$

Apply PEMDAS

5. $(8 + 2)^2 \div 5$

6. Maria says $3 + 4 \times 2 = 14$. Jake says the answer is 11. Who is correct?

★ 3.2 Translating Words into Expressions ★

Learning Goals

- Match math operations to everyday words
- Write algebraic expressions from word phrases
- Understand that order matters for subtraction and division

Words to Math

A **variable** is a letter that stands for a number. You can turn word phrases into math using a variable.

Word Phrase	Expression
A number plus 5	$n+5$
7 less than a number	$n-7$
Twice a number	$2n$
A number divided by 3	$n \div 3$

"Less than" flips the order. "7 less than n" is $n-7$, not $7-n$.

Translate a Phrase

Write an expression for: "Subtract y from 5."

Solution:

1. "Subtract y" means take y away.
2. "From 5" means start with 5.
3. Expression: $5 - y$.

Answer: $5 - y$

TIP

Read the phrase carefully. "5 from y" means $y - 5$. "y from 5" means $5 - y$. The number after "from" comes first.

Translating Words Practice

Write an Expression

1. The sum of 8 and a number k
2. 4 less than a number m
3. Triple a number w, then add 10
4. A number p divided by 6

Match Phrase to Expression

5. Which expression matches "9 more than twice x"?
6.

   A. $2x - 9$ **B.** $9 + 2x$ **C.** $9 \times 2x$ **D.** $2(x + 9)$

7. "Divide 10 by n" and "divide n by 10" give the same expression. True ○ False ○

3.3 Terms, Factors, and Coefficients

Learning Goals

- Identify parts of an expression: terms, factors, coefficients, constants
- Recognize that a group like $(x + 7)$ can act as a single piece

Parts of an Expression

An expression is made of **terms** separated by $+$ or $-$ signs.

Look at $3x + 5y - 2$:

- **Terms**: $3x$, $5y$, and 2. Each chunk is one term.
- **Coefficient**: The number in front of a variable. In $3x$, the coefficient is 3.
- **Constant**: A term with no variable. Here it is 2.
- **Factors**: The pieces multiplied inside a term. In $3x$, the factors are 3 and x.

If you see $2(x + 7)$, the two factors are 2 and $(x + 7)$. The group $(x + 7)$ counts as one factor.

Identify the Parts

Name the terms, coefficients, and constants in $4a + 9 - b$.

Solution:

1. Terms: $4a$, 9, b.

2. Coefficients: 4 (for a) and 1 (for b, since $b = 1 \cdot b$).
3. Constant: 9.

When a variable has no number in front, its coefficient is 1. We just don't write it!

Terms, Factors, and Coefficients Practice

Identify the Parts

1. How many terms are in $7m + 3n - 5$?
2. What is the coefficient of y in $y + 12$?
3. Name the constant in $6k - 8 + 2k$.
4. In the expression $5(x + 3)$, what are the two factors?

True or False

5. In $9x$, the factors are 9 and x. True ○ False ○
6. The expression $4 + 2y$ has two constants. True ○ False ○

3.4 Evaluating Expressions

Learning Goals

- Substitute a number for a variable
- Use the order of operations to compute the value
- Evaluate expressions from real formulas

How to Evaluate

Evaluating means replacing each variable with a number and calculating.

Evaluate $3x + 7$ when $x = 4$:

1. Replace x with 4: $3(4) + 7$
2. Multiply: $12 + 7$
3. Add: 19

Always use parentheses when you substitute. Write $3(4)$, not 34.

Two Variables

Evaluate $2a - b^2$ when $a = 10$ and $b = 3$.

Solution:

1. Substitute: $2(10) - (3)^2$.

2. Exponent: $3^2 = 9$.
3. Multiply: $2(10) = 20$.
4. Subtract: $20 - 9 = 11$.

Answer: 11

TIP

Follow PEMDAS after you substitute. Exponents come before multiplication and addition.

Evaluating Expressions Practice

Evaluate

1. $5n - 3$ when $n = 6$

2. $x^2 + 4$ when $x = 5$

3. $\dfrac{a+b}{2}$ when $a = 8$, $b = 12$

4. $3(m - 4)$ when $m = 9$

Real-World Formulas

5. The perimeter of a rectangle is $P = 2l + 2w$. Find P when $l = 12$ cm and $w = 5$ cm.

6. A phone plan costs $\$20 + \$0.10 \times t$ where t is the number of texts. Find the cost for 150 texts.

★ 3.5 Equivalent Expressions ★

Learning Goals

- Use the distributive property to rewrite expressions
- Combine like terms
- Check equivalence by substituting values

Equivalent Expressions

Two expressions are **equivalent** if they give the same value for every number.

The Distributive Property

$a(b+c) = ab + ac$

$3(x+4) = 3x + 12$

Combining Like Terms

Like terms have the same variable. Add their coefficients.

$5n + 3 + 2n = 7n + 3$

You can check: plug in $n = 2$**. Left:** $5(2) + 3 + 2(2) = 17$**. Right:** $7(2) + 3 = 17$**. Same!**

Simplify an Expression

Simplify: $4(x+5)+3x$

Solution:

1. Distribute: $4x+20+3x$.
2. Combine like terms: $4x+3x=7x$.
3. Result: $7x+20$.

Answer: $7x + 20$

"Think of like terms as matching groups. $5n$ and $2n$ are both "n-groups," so you can put them together: $7n$."

Equivalent Expressions Practice

Simplify

1. $6x + 2x - 4$

2. $2(y + 9)$

3. $3(2m + 1) + 5m$

Equivalence Check

4. Are $4(n + 2)$ and $4n + 8$ equivalent? Test with $n = 3$.

5. $3x + 5x = 8x^2$ True ○ False ○

6. Write an equivalent expression for $10a - 2a + 7$.

3.6 Variables in Real-World Problems

Learning Goals

- Use variables to describe unknown or changing quantities
- Write expressions and equations from real situations
- Understand that a variable can stand for one value or many

Variables Represent Real Quantities

A **variable** is a letter that stands for a number you don't know yet.

One unknown value: A skateboard costs $\$45$ and you have d dollars. After buying it you have $d - 45$ dollars left. Here d is one specific amount — whatever is in your wallet.

Any value in a set: A square has side length s. Its perimeter is $4s$. Here s could be any positive number — the formula works for all of them.

Always say what the variable means. "Let h = number of hours" keeps your work clear.

Write an Expression from a Story

A movie ticket costs $\$12$ per person. Your group also pays $\$6$ for popcorn. Write an expression for the total cost when p people go.

Solution:

1. Tickets: $12 \times p = 12p$.
2. Popcorn (one-time): 6.
3. Total: $12p + 6$.

Answer: $12p + 6$

TIP

Look for what **changes** and what **stays the same**. The changing part gets a variable. The fixed part is a number.

Variables in Real-World Problems Practice

Write an Expression

1. A gym charges $\$25$ to join and $\$10$ per month. Write an expression for the total cost after m months.

2. You have 50 songs and download n more each week. Write an expression for the total after w weeks.

3. A rectangle has length l and width 3. Write an expression for its area.

Choose the Variable

4. A pizza costs $\$14$. You split it equally among friends. What variable do you need, and what is each person's share?

5. In $P = 4s$, the variable s can only be one number. True ◯ False ◯

3.7 Solving One-Step Equations

Learning Goals

- Solve equations of the form $x + p = q$ and $px = q$
- Use inverse operations to isolate the variable
- Check solutions by substituting back

Solving with Inverse Operations

An **equation** says two sides are equal. To solve, undo the operation to get the variable alone.

Addition $\rightarrow$ Subtract

$x + 8 = 15$

Subtract 8 from both sides: $x = 15 - 8 = 7$.

Multiplication $\rightarrow$ Divide

$4x = 36$

Divide both sides by 4: $x = 36 \div 4 = 9$.

Whatever you do to one side, you must do to the other side.

Solve and Check

Solve $x - 5 = 12$.

Solution:

1. Subtraction is the operation. Undo it by adding 5.
2. $x = 12 + 5 = 17$.
3. Check: $17 - 5 = 12$. ✓

Answer: $x = 17$

Always check your answer. Plug it back into the original equation. Both sides should match!

Solving One-Step Equations Practice

Solve Each Equation

1. $y + 9 = 20$
2. $m - 7 = 15$
3. $6k = 54$
4. $\frac{n}{5} = 8$

Word Problems

5. A book costs $\$7$ more than a magazine. The book costs $\$19$. Write and solve an equation for the magazine price m.

6. Three friends split a bill equally and each paid $\$14$. Write and solve an equation for the total bill b.

3.8 Writing Inequalities

Learning Goals

- Write inequalities using $<$, $>$, $\leq$, $\geq$
- Translate phrases like "at least" and "no more than"
- Understand that inequalities have many solutions

Inequality Symbols

An **inequality** compares two values that may not be equal.

Symbol	Meaning	Phrase
$<$	less than	"fewer than," "under"
$>$	greater than	"more than," "over"
$\leq$	less than or equal to	"at most," "no more than"
$\geq$	greater than or equal to	"at least," "no fewer than"

"At least 5" means 5 or more: $x \geq 5$. "At most 5" means 5 or fewer: $x \leq 5$.

Turn Words into an Inequality

A roller coaster requires riders to be at least 48 inches tall. Write an inequality for the height h.

Solution:

1. "At least 48" means 48 or more.
2. Use $\geq$: $h \geq 48$.

Answer: $h \geq 48$

"At least" and "no fewer than" both mean $\geq$. "At most" and "no more than" both mean $\leq$.

Writing Inequalities Practice

Write an Inequality

1. You must be under 13 to get the kids' price. Let a = age.
2. A bag can hold at most 50 pounds. Let w = weight.
3. You need at least $\$20$ to buy the game. Let d = dollars you have.
4. The temperature stayed below 0 degrees. Let t = temperature.

Think Deeper

5. Is $x = 5$ a solution to $x > 5$?
6. The inequality $n \leq 10$ has exactly 10 solutions. True ○ False ○

★ 3.9 Graphing Inequalities on a Number Line ★

Learning Goals

- Graph inequalities on a number line
- Use open and closed circles correctly
- Test values to check if they are solutions

How to Graph an Inequality

Draw a number line. Mark the boundary number. Then shade the direction that makes the inequality true.

- **Open circle** ○: the number is NOT included ($<$ or $>$).
- **Closed circle** ●: the number IS included ($\leq$ or $\geq$).

Example: $x > 3$ $\rightarrow$ open circle at 3, shade right.

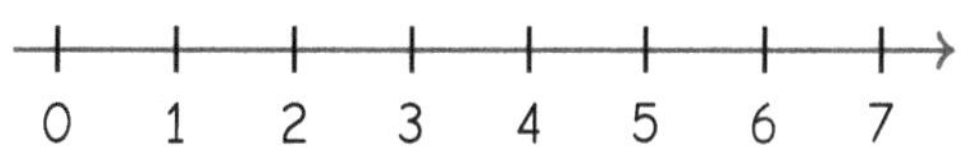

Example: $x \leq 5$ $\rightarrow$ closed circle at 5, shade left.

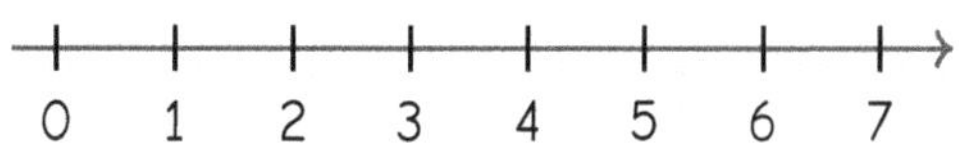

TIP

To check your graph, pick a number in the shaded region and plug it in. If it makes the inequality true, you shaded the right way.

Graphing Inequalities Practice

Describe the Graph

1. $x \geq 2$: Open or closed circle at 2? Shade left or right?
2. $x < 7$: Open or closed circle at 7? Shade left or right?

Test a Value

3. Is $x = 4$ a solution to $x \leq 4$?
4. Is $x = -1$ a solution to $x > 0$?

Write and Graph

5. A pool opens when the temperature is more than 75°F. Write an inequality for t and describe the graph.
6. Write an inequality whose graph has a closed circle at -3 and shades to the left.

3.10 Two Quantities That Change Together

Learning Goals

- Identify independent and dependent variables
- Represent relationships with tables, equations, and graphs
- Describe how one quantity depends on another

Independent and Dependent Variables

When two quantities change together, one **controls** and the other **responds**.

Example: You earn \$8 per hour. The more hours you work, the more money you earn.

- **Independent variable**: hours (h) — you choose this.
- **Dependent variable**: earnings (e) — this depends on hours.
- **Equation**: $e = 8h$.

Hours and Earnings

h (hours)	1	2	3	4	5
e (dollars)	8	16	24	32	40

The independent variable goes on the x-axis. The dependent variable goes on the y-axis.

Identify and Write an Equation

A plant grows 2 cm each week. Write an equation and make a table for the first 4 weeks.

Solution:

1. Independent: weeks (w). Dependent: height (h).
2. Equation: $h = 2w$.
3. Table: $w = 1 \to h = 2;\quad w = 2 \to 4;\quad w = 3 \to 6;\quad w = 4 \to 8.$

TIP

Ask yourself: "Which one do I pick, and which one follows?" The one you pick is independent.

Two Quantities Practice

Identify the Variables

1. A car travels 60 miles per hour. Name the independent and dependent variables.
2. A phone battery loses 5% each hour. Name the independent and dependent variables.

Write and Use Equations

3. A pizza shop charges $\$10$ per pizza. Write an equation for the cost c of p pizzas. Find the cost of 7 pizzas.
4. The equation $d = 3t$ shows how far a turtle walks. Complete: when $t = 5$, $d =$ ______________.
5. In $y = x + 4$, the variable x is the dependent variable. True ○ False ○

CHAPTER

4

Geometry: Area, Surface Area, and Volume

What's Inside

4.1 Area of Triangles

Learning Goals

- Find the area of a triangle using the formula
- Connect triangle area to rectangle area
- Identify the base and height of a triangle

Triangle Area

Every triangle is half of a rectangle.

Area of a Triangle

$$A = \frac{1}{2} \times b \times h$$

- b = **base** — any side of the triangle.
- h = **height** — the perpendicular distance from the base to the opposite vertex.

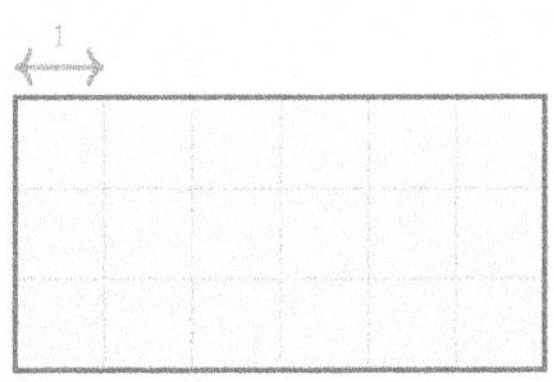

A 6×3 rectangle has area 18. A triangle with the same base and height has area $18 \div 2 = 9$.

The height must be perpendicular (at a right angle) to the base. It is NOT always a side of the triangle.

Find the Area

A triangle has base 10 cm and height 7 cm. Find its area.

Solution:

1. $A = \frac{1}{2} \times 10 \times 7$
2. $A = \frac{1}{2} \times 70 = 35$

Answer: $A = 35$ cm^2

TIP

Multiply the base and height first, then divide by 2. It's easier than multiplying by $\frac{1}{2}$ first.

Area of Triangles Practice

Find the Area

1. Base $= 8$ in, height $= 5$ in.
2. Base $= 12$ cm, height $= 9$ cm.
3. Base $= 3.5$ m, height $= 4$ m.
4. Base $= 6$ ft, height $= 6$ ft.

Apply It

5. A triangular sail has a base of 4 m and a height of 6 m. How much fabric is needed?
6. A triangle with base 10 and height 4 has the same area as one with base 8 and height 5. **True** ○ **False** ○

4.2 Area of Parallelograms and Trapezoids

Learning Goals

- Find the area of parallelograms using base and height
- Find the area of trapezoids using the formula
- Decompose shapes to find area

Area Formulas

Parallelogram

A parallelogram can be cut and rearranged into a rectangle.

$A = b \times h$

The **height** is perpendicular to the base — it is NOT the slanted side.

Trapezoid

A trapezoid has two parallel sides called **bases** (b_1 and b_2).

$A = \frac{1}{2} \times (b_1 + b_2) \times h$

Add the two bases, multiply by the height, then take half.

Find Each Area

Parallelogram

Base $= 9$ cm, height $= 4$ cm.

$A = 9 \times 4 = 36$ cm^2.

Trapezoid

$b_1 = 5$ in, $b_2 = 11$ in, $h = 6$ in.
$A = \frac{1}{2} \times (5 + 11) \times 6 = \frac{1}{2} \times 16 \times 6 = 48$ in^2.

“For a parallelogram, the slanted side is NOT the height. Look for the line that makes a right angle with the base.”

Area Practice

Parallelograms

1. Base $= 7$ m, height $= 3$ m.

2. Base $= 10$ ft, height $= 5.5$ ft.

Trapezoids

3. $b_1 = 4$ cm, $b_2 = 8$ cm, $h = 5$ cm.

4. $b_1 = 3$ in, $b_2 = 9$ in, $h = 4$ in.

Apply It

5. A park is shaped like a trapezoid with parallel sides 40 m and 60 m, and height 30 m. What is the area?

6. A parallelogram with base 6 and height 4 has the same area as a rectangle that is 6 by 4. **True** ○ **False** ○

4.3 Volume of Rectangular Prisms

Learning Goals

- Find the volume of rectangular prisms using $V = lwh$
- Work with fractional edge lengths
- Interpret volume as unit cubes that fit inside

Volume of a Rectangular Prism

Volume measures how much space a 3D shape fills. For a rectangular prism (a box):

Volume

$$V = l \times w \times h$$

- l = length, w = width, h = height.
- Volume is measured in **cubic units** (cm^3, in^3, ft^3).
- Think of it as: how many unit cubes fit inside the box?

You can also find volume in two steps: area of the base $\times$ height. The base is a rectangle, so its area is $l \times w$.

Fractional Edge Lengths

A box is $2\frac{1}{2}$ ft long, 4 ft wide, and 3 ft tall. Find the volume.

Solution:

1. Convert: $2\frac{1}{2} = 2.5$.
2. $V = 2.5 \times 4 \times 3$.
3. $2.5 \times 4 = 10$. Then $10 \times 3 = 30$.

Answer: $V = 30$ ft^3

TIP

When edges are fractions, convert to decimals or improper fractions first. Then multiply step by step.

Volume Practice

Find the Volume

1. $l = 6$ cm, $w = 4$ cm, $h = 5$ cm.
2. $l = 8$ in, $w = 3$ in, $h = 2$ in.
3. $l = 1.5$ m, $w = 2$ m, $h = 4$ m.
4. $l = \frac{1}{2}$ ft, $w = \frac{1}{2}$ ft, $h = \frac{1}{2}$ ft.

Apply It

5. A fish tank is 20 in long, 10 in wide, and 12 in tall. What is its volume?
6. A box has volume 60 cm^3. Its length is 5 cm and width is 4 cm. What is the height?

★ 4.4 Polygons on the Coordinate Plane ★

Learning Goals

- Plot vertices to draw polygons on the coordinate plane
- Find lengths of horizontal and vertical sides using coordinates
- Use absolute value to calculate side lengths

Drawing Shapes with Coordinates

You can draw a polygon by plotting its **vertices** (corners) and connecting them.

Horizontal sides have the same y-coordinate. Their length is the distance between the x-values.
Vertical sides have the same x-coordinate. Their length is the distance between the y-values.

Example: Points $(2, 3)$ and $(2, -1)$ form a vertical side.
Length $= |3 - (-1)| = |4| = 4$ units.

When coordinates cross zero, use absolute value: add the distances from each point to zero. $|3| + |-1| = 4$.

Find the Side Lengths

A rectangle has vertices $A(-3, 2)$, $B(5, 2)$, $C(5, -1)$, $D(-3, -1)$. Find the length and width.

Solution:

1. Side AB is horizontal ($y = 2$). Length $= |5 - (-3)| = 8$ units.
2. Side BC is vertical ($x = 5$). Length $= |2 - (-1)| = 3$ units.

Answer: Length $=$ 8 units, width $=$ 3 units.

“Same y → horizontal side (subtract x-values). Same x → vertical side (subtract y-values). Always use absolute value!”

Polygons on the Coordinate Plane Practice

Find the Side Length

1. Points $(1, 4)$ and $(1, -2)$. What is the distance?
2. Points $(-5, 3)$ and $(3, 3)$. What is the distance?

Plot and Measure

3. A triangle has vertices $(0, 0)$, $(6, 0)$, $(3, 4)$. What is the length of the base along the x-axis?
4. A square has vertices $(2, 2)$, $(2, -2)$, $(-2, -2)$, $(-2, 2)$. What is the side length?

Challenge

5. A rectangle has vertices $(-4, 5)$, $(6, 5)$, $(6, -3)$, $(-4, -3)$. Find the perimeter.

4.5 Finding Area on the Coordinate Plane

Learning Goals

- Find side lengths of polygons using coordinates
- Calculate the area of rectangles and triangles on the coordinate plane
- Break irregular shapes into simpler pieces to find area

Area from Coordinates

Once you know the side lengths from coordinates, use your area formulas:

- **Rectangle:** $A = l \times w$
- **Triangle:** $A = \frac{1}{2} \times b \times h$ (use horizontal base and vertical height)

For **irregular shapes**, break them into rectangles and triangles you know how to measure. Then add the areas together.

Area of a Rectangle on the Plane

A rectangle has vertices $(-2, 1)$, $(4, 1)$, $(4, -3)$, $(-2, -3)$. Find the area.

Solution:

1. Length (horizontal): $|4 - (-2)| = 6$ units.
2. Width (vertical): $|1 - (-3)| = 4$ units.
3. Area $= 6 \times 4 = 24$ sq units.

Answer: 24 **square units**

TIP

I

Finding Area on the Coordinate Plane Practice

Find the Area

1. A rectangle has vertices $(0,0)$, $(5,0)$, $(5,3)$, $(0,3)$. Find the area.
2. A rectangle has vertices $(-3,4)$, $(3,4)$, $(3,-2)$, $(-3,-2)$. Find the area.
3. A right triangle has vertices $(0,0)$, $(8,0)$, $(0,6)$. Find the area.
4. A right triangle has vertices $(1,1)$, $(1,7)$, $(5,1)$. Find the area.

Challenge

5. An L-shaped figure has vertices $(0,0)$, $(6,0)$, $(6,2)$, $(3,2)$, $(3,5)$, $(0,5)$. Split it into two rectangles and find the total area.

★ 4.6 Nets and Surface Area ★

Learning Goals

- Identify nets of 3D shapes (rectangular prisms, triangular prisms, pyramids)
- Find surface area by adding the areas of all faces
- Solve real-world problems involving surface area

What Is a Net?

A **net** is a flat pattern that folds into a 3D shape. Each part of the net becomes one **face** of the solid.

Surface area is the total area of *all* the faces of a 3D shape.

Rectangular Prism (6 faces)

A rectangular prism has 3 pairs of matching faces: SA $= 2lw + 2lh + 2wh$

Triangular Prism (5 faces)

2 triangular bases + 3 rectangular sides.

Think of wrapping a gift box—surface area is how much wrapping paper you need!

Surface Area of a Rectangular Prism

Find the surface area of a box that is 5 cm long, 3 cm wide, and 4 cm tall.

Solution:

1. $\text{SA} = 2lw + 2lh + 2wh$
2. $= 2(5)(3) + 2(5)(4) + 2(3)(4)$
3. $= 30 + 40 + 24 = 94$

Answer: 94 cm^2

*Always label your answer in **square units** (like cm^2 or in^2) because surface area measures flat space, not volume!*

Nets and Surface Area Practice

Surface Area of Rectangular Prisms

1. Find the surface area: $l = 6$ in, $w = 4$ in, $h = 2$ in.
2. A cube has edges of 5 cm. Find the surface area.
3. Find the surface area: $l = 10$ m, $w = 3$ m, $h = 7$ m.

Real-World Problems

4. Maya paints all sides of a wooden crate measuring 2 ft by 3 ft by 4 ft. How many square feet does she paint?

Challenge

5. A triangular prism has two right triangle bases with legs 3 cm and 4 cm and hypotenuse 5 cm. The prism is 10 cm long. Find the total surface area.

CHAPTER

5

Statistics and Data

What's Inside

5.1 Statistical Questions

Learning Goals

- Tell the difference between statistical and non-statistical questions
- Understand that statistical questions expect answers that vary
- Write your own statistical questions to collect data

What Makes a Question Statistical?

A **statistical question** is one where you expect *different* answers from different people or situations.

Statistical

"How many hours do sixth graders sleep each night?"

Different students sleep different amounts, so the answers **vary**.

Not Statistical

"How many hours are in a day?"

There is only one answer: 24. The answer does **not** vary.

If the answer can change from person to person (or time to time), it's a statistical question.

"A quick test: ask yourself, "Would I get different answers if I asked 10 people?" If yes, it's statistical!"

Why Statistical Questions Matter

Scientists, coaches, and businesses all use statistical questions to collect data and make decisions. A coach might ask, "How many free throws does each player make out of 10?" The answers vary, and the coach uses the data to plan practice.

Statistical Questions Practice

Statistical or Not?

1. "What is the capital of France?"
2. "How many pets do students in our class have?"
3. "How tall are the students in sixth grade?"
4. "What is 7×8?"

Challenge

5. Write a statistical question you could ask your classmates. Explain why the answers would vary.

5.2 Describing Data: Center, Spread, and Shape

Learning Goals

- Describe a data set using center, spread, and overall shape
- Identify clusters, gaps, peaks, and outliers
- Explain what these features tell us about the data

Three Ways to Describe Data

When you look at a data set, ask three questions:

Center

Where is the "middle" of the data? This is a typical value. (You'll learn exact ways to find it in the next topic.)

Spread

How spread out are the values? Are they bunched close together or scattered far apart?

Shape

What does the data look like on a graph? Is it symmetric (even on both sides), skewed (stretched to one side), or does it have gaps?

Describing a Data Set

Test scores: $72, 78, 80, 81, 82, 83, 85, 95$.

Solution:

1. **Center:** Most scores are around $80–83$.
2. **Spread:** Scores range from 72 to 95 (range $= 23$).
3. **Shape:** Most values cluster in the $78–85$ range. The 95 is an **outlier** (far from the rest). The 72 is also a bit separated—a small **gap**.

> *An **outlier** is a value that is much higher or lower than the rest. It can pull the center away from the typical values!*

Describing Data Practice

Identify the Feature

1. Data: $10, 11, 12, 12, 13, 13, 14$. Is this data set spread out or bunched together?
2. Data: $3, 5, 6, 7, 7, 8, 25$. Is there an outlier? If so, which value?
3. Data: $20, 22, 23, 23, 24, 24, 24, 25, 26$. Where is the center of this data?

Challenge

4. Two students measured how many pages they read each day for a week. Student A: $10, 12, 11, 13, 12, 11, 12$. Student B: $2, 5, 8, 12, 18, 22, 30$. Which student's data is more spread out? Explain.

★ 5.3 Mean and Median ★

Learning Goals

- Calculate the mean (average) of a data set
- Find the median (middle value) of a data set
- Decide which measure of center is more useful

Two Ways to Find the Center

Mean (Average)

Add all the values, then divide by how many there are.

$$\text{Mean} = \frac{\text{sum of all values}}{\text{number of values}}$$

Median (Middle Value)

Put the values in order from least to greatest. The middle number is the median.

If there are **two** middle numbers, find their average.

Finding Mean and Median

Data: $4, 8, 6, 10, 7$.

Solution:

1. **Mean:** $4 + 8 + 6 + 10 + 7 = 35$. Divide: $35 \div 5 = 7$.
2. **Median:** Order the data: $4, 6, 7, 8, 10$. The middle value is 7.

Answer: Mean = 7, Median = 7

TIP

The mean is pulled toward outliers. If one value is very high or very low, the **median** is a better measure of center.

"Even number of values? Average the two middle numbers! Example: middle values 6 and $8 \rightarrow$ median $= \frac{6+8}{2} = 7$."

Mean and Median Practice

Find the Mean and Median

1. Data: $3, 5, 7, 9, 11$. Find the mean and median.

2. Data: $12, 15, 18, 20$. Find the mean and median.

3. Data: $2, 3, 4, 5, 100$. Find the mean. Is the mean a good description of a "typical" value? Why or why not?

Challenge

4. Five friends scored $80, 85, 90, 92, 88$ on a test. A sixth friend scored 40. How does adding this score change the mean?

5.4 Measures of Spread

Learning Goals

- Find the range, interquartile range (IQR), and mean absolute deviation (MAD)
- Explain what each measure tells us about how spread out data is
- Compare data sets using measures of spread

How Spread Out Is the Data?

Range

Range = greatest value − least value

Simple, but one outlier can make the range huge.

Interquartile Range (IQR)

The IQR measures the spread of the **middle half** of the data.

IQR $= Q3 - Q1$

$Q1$ is the median of the lower half. $Q3$ is the median of the upper half.

Mean Absolute Deviation (MAD)

The MAD tells you how far, on average, each value is from the mean.

Steps: (1) Find the mean. (2) Find each value's distance from the mean. (3) Average those distances.

Finding Range and IQR

Data (in order): $2, 4, 5, 7, 9, 12, 15$.

Solution:

1. **Range:** $15 - 2 = 13$.
2. **Median:** 7 (the 4th value out of 7).
3. $Q1$: Median of $2, 4, 5 = 4$. $Q3$: Median of $9, 12, 15 = 12$.
4. **IQR:** $12 - 4 = 8$.

Answer: **Range** $=$ 13, **IQR** $=$ 8

*A **small** IQR or MAD means the data is consistent. A **large** one means the data is spread out!*

Measures of Spread Practice

Find Range and IQR

1. Data: $10, 14, 18, 22, 26$. Find the range.

2. Data: $3, 5, 7, 8, 10, 12, 14$. Find $Q1$, $Q3$, and the IQR.

Mean Absolute Deviation

3. Data: $4, 6, 8, 10, 12$. The mean is 8. Find the MAD.

4. Data: $10, 10, 10, 10, 10$. What is the MAD?

Challenge

5. Team A scores: $50, 55, 60, 65, 70$. Team B scores: $20, 40, 60, 80, 100$. Both have the same mean (60). Which team is more consistent? Use the range to explain.

5.5 Dot Plots and Histograms

Learning Goals

- Read and create frequency tables
- Read and interpret dot plots and histograms
- Find the mode and choose the best display type

Three Ways to Display Data

Frequency Table

A frequency table lists each value (or interval) and how many times it appears. It is the simplest way to organize raw data.

Dot Plot

A dot plot places a dot above a number line for each data value. It shows **every individual value**.
Best for: **small data sets** where you want to see each value.

Histogram

A histogram groups data into **equal intervals** (bins) and uses bars to show counts. No gaps between bars.
Best for: **large data sets** where individual values are hard to read.

The mode is the value that appears most often. You can spot it quickly in a frequency table or dot plot!

From Data to Frequency Table

Quiz scores: $7, 8, 8, 9, 8, 10, 9, 7, 8, 9$.

Score	Frequency
7	2
8	4
9	3
10	1

Total students: $2 + 4 + 3 + 1 = 10$. Mode: 8 (highest frequency). Range: $10 - 7 = 3$.

TIP

In a histogram, the height of each bar tells you how many values are in that interval. A taller bar = more data points.

Data Display Practice

Frequency Tables

1. Students' shoe sizes: $6, 7, 7, 8, 8, 8, 9, 9, 10$. Make a frequency table and find the mode.

2. A frequency table shows: Red (5), Blue (3), Green (7), Yellow (1). How many responses total? What is the mode?

Dot Plot and Histogram

3. A dot plot of daily high temperatures shows: 68°F (1 dot), 70°F (3 dots), 72°F (4 dots), 74°F (2 dots). What is the mode?

4. A histogram shows test scores: $60–69$ (3), $70–79$ (8), $80–89$ (12), $90–100$ (7). How many students scored 80 or above?

Choose a Display

5. Would you use a dot plot or a histogram for the ages of 500 people at a concert? Explain.

6. You survey 15 classmates about their favorite fruit. Would a frequency table or histogram be the best first step? Why?

5.6 Box Plots

Learning Goals

- Find the five-number summary of a data set
- Read and interpret box plots
- Compare two groups using box plots

The Five-Number Summary

A **box plot** (box-and-whisker plot) displays five key values:

1. **Minimum** — the smallest value
2. $Q1$ (first quartile) — median of the lower half
3. **Median** ($Q2$) — the middle value
4. $Q3$ (third quartile) — median of the upper half
5. **Maximum** — the largest value

The **box** stretches from $Q1$ to $Q3$. A line inside marks the median. The **whiskers** extend to the min and max.

The box contains the middle 50% of the data. A longer box means more variability in the middle half.

Reading and Comparing Box Plots

Two classes took the same test.

	Min	$Q1$	Median	$Q3$	Max
Class A	60	72	80	88	98
Class B	50	65	78	90	100

Solution:

1. **Center:** Class A's median (80) is slightly higher than Class B's (78).
2. **Spread:** Class A's IQR $= 88 - 72 = 16$. Class B's IQR $= 90 - 65 = 25$.
3. **Conclusion:** Class A scored slightly higher and was **more consistent** (tighter box).

> *Wider box = more spread. When comparing two box plots, look at* ***overlap****. If the boxes barely overlap, the groups are clearly different.*

Box Plots Practice

Read the Box Plot

1. A box plot shows: min $= 40$, $Q1 = 55$, median $= 65$, $Q3 = 80$, max $= 95$. What percent of data falls between 55 and 80?

2. Using the same box plot, the left whisker goes from 40 to 55. What does this whisker represent?

Build a Five-Number Summary

3. Data: $5, 8, 12, 15, 20, 24, 28$. Find the five-number summary.

Compare Two Groups

4. Team X: median $= 75$, IQR $= 10$. Team Y: median $= 75$, IQR $= 30$. Both medians are equal. What does the IQR tell you?

5. Store A daily customers: min $= 30$, $Q1 = 45$, median $= 60$, $Q3 = 70$, max $= 90$. Store B: min $= 50$, $Q1 = 55$, median $= 58$, $Q3 = 62$, max $= 68$. Which store has more predictable traffic?

★ 5.7 Summarizing Data and Making Comparisons ★

Learning Goals

- Summarize a data set using center and spread together
- Compare two data sets using numbers and graphs
- Support claims about data with evidence

Putting It All Together

A good data summary uses **both** center and spread:

- **Center** (mean or median) tells you what is typical.
- **Spread** (range or IQR) tells you how consistent the data is.

When **comparing two groups**, ask:

1. Which group has a higher center?
2. Which group is more spread out?
3. Do the data sets overlap a lot or a little?

Use the median and IQR when data is skewed or has outliers. Use the mean and range when data is roughly symmetric with no extremes.

Comparing Two Teams

Team A test scores: mean $= 82$, IQR $= 8$. Team B: mean $= 78$, IQR $= 22$.

Solution:

1. **Center:** Team A's mean (82) is higher than Team B's (78).
2. **Spread:** Team A's IQR is 8 (very consistent). Team B's IQR is 22 (much more spread).
3. **Conclusion:** Team A scored higher on average *and* was more consistent.

> *Always back up your claims with numbers! Don't just say "Group A did better." Say why: "Group A's median was 10 points higher and its IQR was half as wide."*

Summarizing Data Practice

Summarize the Data

1. Data: $15, 18, 20, 22, 25$. Find the mean and range, then write one sentence summarizing the data.
2. Data: $5, 5, 6, 6, 6, 7, 7, 50$. Would you use the mean or median? Explain.

Compare Two Groups

3. Class A: median $= 85$, IQR $= 8$. Class B: median $= 80$, IQR $= 20$. Which class performed better and more consistently?
4. Store A daily sales: mean $= \$400$, range $= \$200$. Store B: mean $= \$400$, range $= \$600$. The means are equal. What does the range tell you?

Challenge

5. A soccer team scored per game: $1, 2, 2, 3, 3, 3, 4$. A basketball team scored: $60, 65, 70, 75, 80, 85, 90$. Jayden says the basketball team is "more spread out" because their range (30) is bigger than the soccer team's (3). Do you agree?

★ 5.8 Stem-and-Leaf Plots ★

Learning Goals

- Organize data into a stem-and-leaf plot
- Read a stem-and-leaf plot to find mean, median, mode, and range
- Compare data sets using back-to-back stem-and-leaf plots

What Is a Stem-and-Leaf Plot?

A **stem-and-leaf plot** splits each number into a **stem** (all digits except the last) and a **leaf** (the last digit).

Example: Data: $23, 25, 31, 34, 34, 38, 42, 45.$

Stem	Leaves
2	3 5
3	1 4 4 8
4	2 5

Leaves must be in order from least to greatest. Always include a key: $3|4$ **means** $34.$

Reading a Stem-and-Leaf Plot

Use the plot above to find the median, mode, and range.

Solution:

1. 8 data points. Median: average of 4th and 5th values $= (34 + 34)/2 = 34$.
2. Mode: 34 (appears twice).
3. Range: $45 - 23 = 22$.

Answer: Median $= 34$, **Mode** $= 34$, **Range** $= 22$

A stem-and-leaf plot keeps every data value visible — unlike a histogram, which only shows counts per interval!

Stem-and-Leaf Plot Practice

Build and Read

1. Organize this data into a stem-and-leaf plot: $15, 18, 22, 24, 27, 31, 35$.
2. Using the plot you built, find the median and range.

Interpret

3. A stem-and-leaf plot shows: Stem 5: $0\ 2\ 5\ 8$; Stem 6: $1\ 3\ 3\ 7$; Stem 7: $0\ 4$. How many data points? What is the mode?

Challenge

4. Test scores: $72, 78, 81, 83, 85, 88, 90, 92, 95, 98$. Build a stem-and-leaf plot and find the median.

Answer Key

★ Check Your Answers! ★

Try each problem first, then look here to check your work.
It's OK to make mistakes — that's how we learn ★

Chapter 1

Section 1.1

1. 6 to 10, $6:10$, $\frac{6}{10}$
2. 10 to 6, $10:6$, $\frac{10}{6}$
3. 6 to 16, $6:16$, $\frac{6}{16}$
4. $3:5$
5. $\frac{8}{14}$
6. $9:15$
7. 8 tablets
8. 9 children

Explanations

1. Apples first, then oranges.

2. Oranges first, then apples.

3. Total $= 6 + 10 = 16$. This is a part-to-whole ratio.

6. Total games $= 9 + 6 = 15$.

7. $20 \div 5 = 4$ groups. $4 \times 2 = 8$ tablets.

8. $21 \div 7 = 3$ groups. $3 \times 3 = 9$ children.

Section 1.2

1. $6 : 5$
2. $4 : 1$
3. $3 : 8$
4. $3 : 5$
5. 15 boys
6. 48 rows of corn
7. Answers will vary.
8. 20 practice days and 4 game days

Explanations

4. Non-raisins $= 8 - 3 = 5$.

5. Total parts $= 3 + 5 = 8$. Each part $= 40 \div 8 = 5$. Boys $= 3 \times 5 = 15$.

6. Total parts $= 4 + 1 = 5$. Each part $= 60 \div 5 = 12$. Corn $= 4 \times 12 = 48$.

7. Example: For every 2 rainy days, there are 7 sunny days.

8. Total parts $= 5 + 1 = 6$. Each part $= 24 \div 6 = 4$. Practice $= 5 \times 4 = 20$. Games $= 1 \times 4 = 4$.

Section 1.3

1. Rate
2. Ratio
3. Rate
4. Ratio
5. $\frac{180 \text{ miles}}{3 \text{ hours}}$ or 180 miles per 3 hours
6. $\frac{500 \text{ toys}}{4 \text{ days}}$ or 500 toys per 4 days
7. The cyclist is faster.
8. Answers will vary.

Explanations

1 Touchdowns and games are different units.

2 Both are shirts (same unit).

3 Calories and granola bars are different units.

4 Both describe people — this is part-to-whole.

7 Runner: $12 \div 6 = 2$ minutes per lap. Cyclist: $8 \div 6 \approx 1.33$ minutes per lap. The cyclist takes less time per lap.

8 Examples: miles per hour while driving, dollars per gallon of gas, songs per hour on a playlist.

Section 1.4

1 $15 per month

2 30 miles per gallon

3 $8 per hour

4 The 20-pack

5 Service A

6 Plan Y

Explanations

1 Divide: $\$45 \div 3 = \$15$ per 1 month.

2 $240 \div 8 = 30$ miles per 1 gallon.

3 $\$56 \div 7 = \$8$ per 1 hour.

4 12-pack: $\$5.40 \div 12 = \$0.45$ each. 20-pack: $\$8.00 \div 20 = \$0.40$ each.

5 A per month: $\$108 \div 12 = \$9$. B is $\$10$ per month. $\$9 < \$10$.

6 X: $\$150 \div 5 = \$30$ per line. Y: $\$200 \div 8 = \$25$ per line.

Section 1.5

1 4, 20, 10

2 6, 28, 15

3 Yes

4 No

5 8 cups of yogurt

6 60 students

7 6 cups blue, 27 cups white

Explanations

1 Row 2: $\times 2 \rightarrow 4$. Row 3: $8 \div 2 = 4$, so $\times 4 \rightarrow 20$. Row 4: $\times 5 \rightarrow 10$.

2 Row 2: $\times 2 \rightarrow 6$. Row 3: $12 \div 3 = 4$, so $\times 4 \rightarrow 28$. Row 4: $\times 5 \rightarrow 15$.

3 Both simplify to $2:3$. $(6 \div 3 = 2, 9 \div 3 = 3)$ and $(14 \div 7 = 2, 21 \div 7 = 3)$.

4 $5 \times 3 = 15$ but $8 \times 3 = 24 \neq 20$.

5 $12 \div 3 = 4$. Yogurt: $2 \times 4 = 8$.

6 $35 \div 7 = 5$. Boys: $5 \times 5 = 25$. Total: $25 + 35 = 60$.

7 Total parts $= 2 + 9 = 11$. Each part $= 33 \div 11 = 3$. Blue $= 2 \times 3 = 6$. White $= 9 \times 3 = 27$.

Section 1.6

1 $(1,30), (2,60), (3,90), (4,120)$ 2 Yes 3 $2:5$ 4 Line A 5 False

Explanations

1 Multiply 30 by each hour: $2 \times 30 = 60$, $3 \times 30 = 90$, $4 \times 30 = 120$.

2 $1:3 = 3:9$ — multiply both by 3.

3 Look at any point: $x = 2$, $y = 5$, so the ratio is $2:5$. Check: $4:10$ simplifies to $2:5$ too.

4 Line A rises 4 for every 1, which is faster than 3 for every 1.

5 Equivalent ratios always form a *straight* line through the origin $(0,0)$.

Section 1.7

1 $\frac{60}{100} = \frac{3}{5}$; 0.60 2 15% 3 75% 4 \$53 5 \$5 6 \$42

Explanations

1 60% means 60 out of 100. Simplify: $60 \div 20 = 3$, $100 \div 20 = 5$. Decimal: $60 \div 100 = 0.60$.

2 Multiply the decimal by 100: $0.15 \times 100 = 15\%$.

3 $\frac{3}{4} = \frac{75}{100} = 75\%$.

4 Tax: $0.06 \times \$50 = \$3$. Total: $\$50 + \$3 = \$53$.

5 20% of \$25: $0.20 \times 25 = \$5$.

6 Discount: $0.30 \times \$60 = \$18$. Sale price: $\$60 - \$18 = \$42$.

Section 1.8

1 \$2.10 | 2 \$9 | 3 \$42 | 4 \$30 | 5 \$70 | 6 \$150

Explanations

1 $0.06 \times \$35 = \$2.10$.

2 $0.20 \times \$45 = \$9$.

3 Discount: $0.30 \times \$60 = \$18$. Sale price: $\$60 - \$18 = \$42$.

4 $I = 200 \times 0.05 \times 3 = \$30$.

5 Markup: $0.40 \times \$50 = \$20$. Selling price: $\$50 + \$20 = \$70$.

6 $I = 1{,}000 \times 0.03 \times 5 = \$150$.

Section 1.9

1 420 miles | 2 8 cups red, 28 cups white | 3 \$20, \$40, \$60 | 4 40 km | 5 15 bags

Explanations

1. Unit rate: $180 \div 3 = 60$ mph. In 7 hours: $60 \times 7 = 420$.

2. Total parts: 9. Each part: $36 \div 9 = 4$. Red: $2 \times 4 = 8$. White: $7 \times 4 = 28$.

3. Total parts: 6. Each part: $\$120 \div 6 = \$20$. Shares: \$20, \$40, \$60.

4. $8 \times 5 = 40$ km.

5. $4 \times 5 = 20$, so $3 \times 5 = 15$.

Section 1.10

1. 60 inches
2. 4 hours
3. 3,000 meters
4. 2.5 kg
5. 2 hours 15 minutes
6. 90 inches

Explanations

1. 1 foot = 12 inches. Bigger to smaller → multiply: $5 \times 12 = 60$.

2. 1 hour = 60 minutes. Smaller to bigger → divide: $240 \div 60 = 4$.

3. 1 km = 1,000 m. Bigger to smaller → multiply: $3 \times 1{,}000 = 3{,}000$.

4. 1 kg = 1,000 g. Smaller to bigger → divide: $2{,}500 \div 1{,}000 = 2.5$.

5. Divide: $135 \div 60 = 2$ with remainder 15. So 2 full hours and 15 minutes left over.

6. $2.5 \times 36 = 90$.

Section 1.11

1. (a) need, (b) want, (c) need, (d) want
2. \$12
3. Yes
4. \$30
5. No interest charges

Explanations

1. Rent and groceries are necessary for survival. Sneakers and streaming are nice to have but not essential.

2. $0.20 \times \$60 = \$12$.

3. $10 \times \$12 = \$120 > \$100$. He can buy the bike and have \$20 left.

4. $0.15 \times \$200 = \$30$. Now you owe $\$200 + \$30 = \$230$.

5. A debit card uses money already in your account, so there is no risk of interest charges or building debt.

Section 1.12

1. Proportional
2. Non-proportional
3. Yes, $k = 4$
4. No
5. Yes, $k = 0.60$

Explanations

1 Form $y = kx$ with $k = 7$. No added constant, passes through $(0, 0)$.

2 There is a $+1$, so the line does not pass through $(0, 0)$.

3 $4/1 = 4$, $8/2 = 4$, $12/3 = 4$. The ratio is constant.

4 Cost $= 2 \times$ miles $+ 3$. The base fee means the graph does not start at $(0, 0)$.

5 0 pounds costs $\$0$. Each pound adds $\$0.60$. Cost $= 0.60w$.

Section 1.13

1 \$80 | 2 40% | 3 Plan A earns more | 4 \$9 in interest | 5 \$50

Explanations

1 $\$200 - (\$25 + \$60 + \$35) = \$200 - \$120 = \$80$.

2 $\$80/\$200 = 0.40 = 40\%$.

3 A: $I = 100 \times 0.03 \times 2 = \$6$. B: $I = 100 \times 0.05 \times 1 = \$5$.

4 $I = 75 \times 0.04 \times 3 = \$9$. By buying shoes, you miss earning $\$9$.

5 She gives up $5 \times \$10 = \$50$ in earnings.

Chapter 2

Section 2.1

1. 2
2. $\frac{6}{5}$ or $1\frac{1}{5}$
3. $\frac{5}{4}$ or $1\frac{1}{4}$
4. $\frac{2}{3}$
5. 15
6. $\frac{7}{16}$
7. 6 scoops
8. $2\frac{1}{2}$ pieces

1. 4 walls; yes, exactly enough

Explanations

1. $\frac{1}{2} \times \frac{4}{1} = \frac{4}{2} = 2$

2. $\frac{3}{5} \times \frac{2}{1} = \frac{6}{5}$

3. $\frac{5}{6} \times \frac{3}{2} = \frac{15}{12} = \frac{5}{4}$

4. $\frac{4}{9} \times \frac{3}{2} = \frac{12}{18} = \frac{2}{3}$

5. $\frac{3}{1} \times \frac{5}{1} = 15$

6. $\frac{7}{8} \times \frac{1}{2} = \frac{7}{16}$

7. $\frac{3}{4} \div \frac{1}{8} = \frac{3}{4} \times \frac{8}{1} = \frac{24}{4} = 6$

8. $\frac{5}{6} \div \frac{1}{3} = \frac{5}{6} \times \frac{3}{1} = \frac{15}{6} = \frac{5}{2} = 2\frac{1}{2}$

1 $\frac{2}{3} \div \frac{1}{6} = \frac{2}{3} \times \frac{6}{1} = \frac{12}{3} = 4$ walls. That's exactly 4, so yes!

Section 2.2

1 63 | 2 36 | 3 78 | 4 52 | 5 63 R 13 | 6 84 R 25 | 7 10 buses | 8 204 cars per hour | 1 206 R 15

Explanations

1 $12 \times 63 = 756$

2 $27 \times 36 = 972$

3 $16 \times 78 = 1{,}248$

4 $45 \times 52 = 2{,}340$

5 $14 \times 63 = 882$; $895 - 882 = 13$

6 $38 \times 84 = 3{,}192$; $3{,}217 - 3{,}192 = 25$

7 $342 \div 36 = 9$ R 18. You need 10 buses because the remaining 18 students still need a bus.

8 $2{,}856 \div 14 = 204$

1 A three-digit quotient would mean at least $23 \times 100 = 2{,}300$ and up to $23 \times 999 = 22{,}977$. Since $4{,}753$ is bigger than $2{,}300$ but less than $23{,}000$, the quotient is a three-digit... wait: $23 \times 200 = 4{,}600$ and $23 \times 210 = 4{,}830 > 4{,}753$. So quotient is between 200 and 210. Actually $23 \times 206 = 4{,}738$, remainder 15. The quotient IS three digits: 206.

> Section 2.3

1 21.719 2 36.35 3 72.544 4 15.937 5 25.83 6 0.035 7 22.8
8 13 9 $\$9.22$ 10 13.2 seconds 1 0.0006

Explanations

5 $63 \times 41 = 2{,}583$; 2 decimal places

6 $7 \times 5 = 35$; 3 decimal places

7 $91.2 \div 4 = 22.8$

8 $156 \div 12 = 13$

9 $3 \times 2.49 = 7.47$; $7.47 + 1.75 = 9.22$

10 $52.8 \div 4 = 13.2$

1 $12 \times 5 = 60$. Total decimal places: $3 + 2 = 5$. So 60 with 5 decimal places $= 0.00060 = 0.0006$.

> Section 2.4

1 8 | 2 18 | 3 14 | 4 25 | 5 20 | 6 18 | 7 24 | 8 35 | 9 6 bags

0 24 minutes | 2 True | 4 False

Explanations

1 Factors of 16: $1, 2, 4, 8, 16$. Factors of 40: $1, 2, 4, 5, 8, 10, 20, 40$.

2 $36 = 2^2 \times 3^2$, $54 = 2 \times 3^3$. Shared: $2 \times 3^2 = 18$.

3 Common factors: $1, 2, 7, 14$. Greatest is 14.

4 $100 = 2^2 \times 5^2$, $75 = 3 \times 5^2$. Shared: $5^2 = 25$.

5 Multiples of 4: $4, 8, 12, 16, 20, \ldots$; multiples of 10: $10, 20, \ldots$

6 Multiples of 6: $6, 12, 18$; multiples of 9: $9, 18$.

7 $8 = 2^3$, $12 = 2^2 \times 3$. LCM $= 2^3 \times 3 = 24$.

8 5 and 7 share no common factors, so LCM $= 5 \times 7 = 35$.

9 GCF$(30, 48) = 6$. Each bag: 5 pencils, 8 erasers.

10 LCM$(12, 8) = 24$.

> Section 2.5

1 $4(4+7)$ 2 $15(3+2)$ 3 $7(3+5)$ 4 $18(3+2)$ 5 318 6 \$96

Explanations

1 GCF of 16 and 28 is 4. $16 \div 4 = 4$, $28 \div 4 = 7$.

2 GCF of 45 and 30 is 15. $45 \div 15 = 3$, $30 \div 15 = 2$.

3 GCF of 21 and 35 is 7. $21 \div 7 = 3$, $35 \div 7 = 5$.

4 GCF of 54 and 36 is 18. $54 \div 18 = 3$, $36 \div 18 = 2$.

5 $6 \times 53 = 6(50+3) = 300 + 18 = 318$.

6 $12 \times 8 = (10+2) \times 8 = 80 + 16 = 96$.

> Section 2.6

1 -200 2 $-8°$ 3 2 4 -10 5 3 6 $15 + (-20) = -5$; you owe \$5

Explanations

1 Below sea level is negative.

2 Below zero means negative: -8.

3 Different signs: $5 - 3 = 2$. The positive number is bigger, so the answer is positive.

4. Same signs: $6 + 4 = 10$. Both negative, so -10.

5. Different signs: $10 - 7 = 3$. The positive number is bigger, so positive.

6. Spending is negative. $15 - 20 = -5$. A negative balance means you owe money.

Section 2.7

1. -9
2. 12
3. 15
4. 8
5. Account A
6. May
7. True

Explanations

1. Same distance, other side.

2. Flip the sign.

3. 15 units from zero.

4. Already positive, 8 units from zero.

5. $|-45| = 45 > |-30| = 30$. Account A owes more.

6. $|-200| = 200$ and $|150| = 150$. May had a bigger change from $\$0$.

7. $|-6| = 6$ and $|5| = 5$. Since $6 > 5$, the statement is true.

Section 2.8

1 Between 0 and 1 | 2 Between -3 and -2 | 3 Between -2 and -1 | 4 -3.5 | 5 $-1, -\frac{1}{2}, \frac{1}{4}, 0.75$ | 6 True

Explanations

1 $\frac{1}{2} = 0.5$, which is halfway between 0 and 1, to the right of 0.

2 -2.25 is negative, so left of 0. It is 0.25 past -2 toward -3.

3 $\frac{5}{3} = 1\frac{2}{3} \approx 1.67$. So $-\frac{5}{3}$ is between -2 and -1.

4 $|-3.5| = 3.5$ and $|2.8| = 2.8$. Since $3.5 > 2.8$, -3.5 is farther from 0.

5 Convert: $-1, -0.5, 0.25, 0.75$. Left to right on the number line.

6 $-\frac{1}{2} = -0.5$. They are the same rational number written differently.

Section 2.9

1 IV | 2 II | 3 $(2, 5)$ | 4 $(6, 1)$ | 5 $(3, -4)$ | 6 True

Explanations

1 x is positive, y is negative $\rightarrow$ Quadrant IV.

2 x is negative, y is positive $\rightarrow$ Quadrant II.

3. Flip the y-coordinate: -5 becomes 5. The x stays the same.

4. Flip the x-coordinate: -6 becomes 6. The y stays the same.

5. First reflection: $(-3, -4)$. Second reflection: $(3, -4)$. Both signs flipped.

6. When $x = 0$, the point is on the y-axis, no matter what y is.

Section 2.10

1. $<$ 2. $>$ 3. $=$ 4. $>$ 5. $-8, -1, 0, 3, 5$ 6. Tuesday

Explanations

1. -7 is farther left on the number line, so $-7 < -3$.

2. 0 is to the right of every negative number.

3. They are the same number.

4. Any positive number is greater than any negative number.

5. Place on a number line: leftmost is least, rightmost is greatest.

6. $-9 < -4$, so Tuesday was colder. Farther below zero means colder.

Section 2.11

1 7 | 2 8 | 3 10 | 4 8 | 5 8 blocks | 6 12 units

Explanations

1 Same x. $|4-(-3)| = |4+3| = 7$ units.

2 Same y. $|-5-3| = |-8| = 8$ units.

3 Same $x = 0$. $|-6-4| = |-10| = 10$ units.

4 Same x. $|-1-(-9)| = |-1+9| = 8$ units.

5 Same x. $|5-(-3)| = |8| = 8$ blocks.

6 Same y. $|-7-5| = |-12| = 12$ units.

> Section 2.12

1 -14 | 2 -5 | 3 -6 | 4 7 | 5 -35 feet | 6 -4 yards

Explanations

1 Same signs: $6+8=14$, both negative $\rightarrow -14$.

2 Different signs: $12-7=5$. Bigger absolute value is negative $\rightarrow -5$.

3 $9+(-15)=-6$.

4 $-3 + 10 = 7$. Subtracting -10 is adding 10.

5 $-20 + (-15) = -35$.

6 $8 + (-12) = -4$. The team lost 4 yards overall.

Section 2.13

1 -35 2 24 3 -8 4 8 5 $-\$15$ 6 -4°F per hour

Explanations

1 Different signs → negative.

2 Same signs → positive.

3 Different signs → negative.

4 Same signs → positive.

5 $(-3) \times 5 = -15$. The stock lost $\$15$ total.

6 $(-24) \div 6 = -4$. It dropped 4 degrees each hour.

Chapter 3

Section 3.1

1. 7^3 2. 2^5 3. 64 4. 70 5. 20 6. Jake

Explanations

1. The base 7 is multiplied 3 times.

2. The base 2 is multiplied 5 times.

3. $4 \times 4 = 16$, then $16 \times 4 = 64$.

4. Exponent: $10^2 = 100$. Multiply: $6 \times 5 = 30$. Subtract: $100 - 30 = 70$.

5. Parentheses: $8 + 2 = 10$. Exponent: $10^2 = 100$. Divide: $100 \div 5 = 20$.

6. Multiply first: $4 \times 2 = 8$. Then add: $3 + 8 = 11$. Maria added before multiplying.

Section 3.2

1. $8 + k$ 2. $m - 4$ 3. $3w + 10$ 4. $p \div 6$ 6. B 7. False

Explanations

1. "Sum" means addition: $8 + k$.

2. "Less than" means subtract from m: $m - 4$.

3. "Triple" means $3 \times w = 3w$. Then add 10.

4. "Divided by" puts p on top: $p \div 6$.

6. "Twice x" is $2x$. "9 more" means add 9: $9 + 2x$.

7. $10 \div n \neq n \div 10$. Order matters in division.

Section 3.3

1. 3
2. 1
3. 8
4. 5 and $(x+3)$
5. True
6. False

Explanations

1. The terms are $7m$, $3n$, and 5.

2. y means $1 \cdot y$, so the coefficient is 1.

3. 8 is the only term without a variable.

4. 5 is multiplied by the group $(x+3)$.

5. $9x$ means $9 \times x$, so 9 and x are factors.

6. 4 is a constant, but $2y$ is a variable term, not a constant.

Section 3.4

1 27 | 2 29 | 3 10 | 4 15 | 5 34 cm | 6 \$35

Explanations

1 $5(6) - 3 = 30 - 3 = 27.$

2 $5^2 + 4 = 25 + 4 = 29.$

3 $(8 + 12) \div 2 = 20 \div 2 = 10.$

4 $3(9 - 4) = 3(5) = 15.$

5 $2(12) + 2(5) = 24 + 10 = 34$ cm.

6 $20 + 0.10(150) = 20 + 15 = 35$ dollars.

Section 3.5

1 $8x - 4$ | 2 $2y + 18$ | 3 $11m + 3$ | 4 Yes | 5 False | 6 $8a + 7$

Explanations

1 Combine like terms: $6x + 2x = 8x.$

2 Distribute: $2 \times y + 2 \times 9.$

3 Distribute: $6m + 3 + 5m.$ Combine: $11m + 3.$

4. $4(3+2) = 4(5) = 20$. $4(3) + 8 = 12 + 8 = 20$. Same result.

5. $3x + 5x = 8x$, not $8x^2$. You add coefficients, not multiply the variable.

6. Combine: $10a - 2a = 8a$. The constant stays.

Section 3.6

1. $25 + 10m$
2. $50 + nw$
3. $3l$
4. Let f = number of friends. Each pays $14 \div f$ dollars.
5. False

Explanations

1. Fixed fee: 25. Monthly cost: $10m$. Total: $25 + 10m$.

2. Start with 50, add n songs for w weeks: $50 + nw$.

3. Area = length × width $= l \times 3 = 3l$.

4. The unknown is how many friends share, so use f.

5. s is the side length. It can be any positive number — the formula works for every square.

Section 3.7

1. $y = 11$
2. $m = 22$
3. $k = 9$
4. $n = 40$
5. $m + 7 = 19$, so $m = 12$

6 $\frac{b}{3} = 14$, so $b = 42$

Explanations

1 Subtract 9: $y = 20 - 9 = 11$.

2 Add 7: $m = 15 + 7 = 22$.

3 Divide by 6: $k = 54 \div 6 = 9$.

4 Multiply by 5: $n = 8 \times 5 = 40$.

5 Subtract 7: $m = 19 - 7 = 12$. The magazine costs $\$12$.

6 Multiply by 3: $b = 14 \times 3 = 42$.

Section 3.8

1 $a < 13$ 2 $w \leq 50$ 3 $d \geq 20$ 4 $t < 0$ 5 No 6 False

Explanations

1 "Under 13" means less than 13: $a < 13$.

2 "At most 50" means 50 or less: $w \leq 50$.

3 "At least 20" means 20 or more: $d \geq 20$.

4 "Below 0" means less than 0: $t < 0$.

5 $5 > 5$ is false. 5 is not greater than itself. It would be a solution to $x \geq 5$.

6 $n \leq 10$ has infinitely many solutions: $10, 9.5, 0, -3, \ldots$ any number that is 10 or less.

> Section 3.9

1 Closed circle at 2, shade right

2 Open circle at 7, shade left

3 Yes

4 No

5 $t > 75$; open circle at 75, shade right

6 $x \leq -3$

Explanations

1 $\geq$ includes 2 (closed) and means greater (right).

2 $<$ does not include 7 (open) and means less (left).

3 $4 \leq 4$ is true because 4 equals 4, and $\leq$ includes equality.

4 $-1 > 0$ is false. -1 is to the left of 0.

5 "More than 75" means > 75. Not equal, so open circle.

6 Closed circle means $\leq$ or $\geq$. Shading left means less than: $x \leq -3$.

> Section 3.10

1 Independent: hours (t); Dependent: distance (d)

2 Independent: hours (h); Dependent: battery left (b)

3 $c = 10p$; cost is \$70

4 15

5 False

Explanations

1 You choose how long to drive. Distance depends on time: $d = 60t$.

2 Battery depends on how many hours have passed.

3 $c = 10(7) = 70$ dollars.

4 $d = 3(5) = 15$.

5 x is independent (you choose it). y depends on x.

Chapter 4

Section 4.1

1 20 in^2

2 54 cm^2

3 7 m^2

4 18 ft^2

5 12 m^2

6 True

Explanations

1 $\frac{1}{2} \times 8 \times 5 = 20$.

2. $\frac{1}{2} \times 12 \times 9 = 54.$

3. $\frac{1}{2} \times 3.5 \times 4 = 7.$

4. $\frac{1}{2} \times 6 \times 6 = 18.$

5. $\frac{1}{2} \times 4 \times 6 = 12$ m^2 of fabric.

6. Both give $\frac{1}{2} \times 10 \times 4 = 20$ and $\frac{1}{2} \times 8 \times 5 = 20.$

Section 4.2

1. 21 m^2
2. 55 ft^2
3. 30 cm^2
4. 24 in^2
5. 1,500 m^2
6. True

Explanations

1. $A = 7 \times 3 = 21.$

2. $A = 10 \times 5.5 = 55.$

3. $\frac{1}{2}(4+8)(5) = \frac{1}{2}(60) = 30.$

4. $\frac{1}{2}(3+9)(4) = \frac{1}{2}(48) = 24.$

5. $\frac{1}{2}(40+60)(30) = \frac{1}{2}(3000) = 1500.$

6. Both use $A = b \times h = 24.$ Same formula, same area.

Section 4.3

1 120 cm^3 2 48 in^3 3 12 m^3 4 $\frac{1}{8}\text{ ft}^3$ 5 $2{,}400\text{ in}^3$ 6 3 cm

Explanations

1 $6 \times 4 \times 5 = 120.$

2 $8 \times 3 \times 2 = 48.$

3 $1.5 \times 2 = 3.$ Then $3 \times 4 = 12.$

4 $\frac{1}{2} \times \frac{1}{2} \times \frac{1}{2} = \frac{1}{8}.$

5 $20 \times 10 \times 12 = 2400.$

6 Base area: $5 \times 4 = 20.$ Height: $60 \div 20 = 3$ cm.

Section 4.4

1 6 units 2 8 units 3 6 units 4 4 units 5 36 units

Explanations

1 $|4 - (-2)| = |6| = 6.$

2 $|3 - (-5)| = |8| = 8.$

3. $|6-0| = 6$. The base runs from $(0,0)$ to $(6,0)$.

4. $|2-(-2)| = 4$. Each side is 4 units long.

5. Length: $|6-(-4)| = 10$. Width: $|5-(-3)| = 8$. Perimeter: $2(10)+2(8) = 36$.

Section 4.5

1. 15 sq units
2. 36 sq units
3. 24 sq units
4. 12 sq units
5. 21 sq units

Explanations

1. $5 \times 3 = 15$.

2. Length: $|3-(-3)| = 6$. Width: $|4-(-2)| = 6$. Area: $6 \times 6 = 36$.

3. Base $= 8$, height $= 6$. Area $= \frac{1}{2} \times 8 \times 6 = 24$.

4. Base $= |5-1| = 4$. Height $= |7-1| = 6$. Area $= \frac{1}{2} \times 4 \times 6 = 12$.

5. Bottom rectangle: $6 \times 2 = 12$. Top-left rectangle: $3 \times 3 = 9$. Total: $12+9 = 21$.

Section 4.6

1. 88 in^2
2. 150 cm^2
3. 242 m^2
4. 52 ft^2
5. 132 cm^2

Explanations

1. $2(6)(4) + 2(6)(2) + 2(4)(2) = 48 + 24 + 16 = 88.$

2. A cube has 6 equal faces: $6 \times 5^2 = 6 \times 25 = 150.$

3. $2(10)(3) + 2(10)(7) + 2(3)(7) = 60 + 140 + 42 = 242.$

4. $2(2)(3) + 2(2)(4) + 2(3)(4) = 12 + 16 + 24 = 52.$

5. 2 triangles: $2 \times \frac{1}{2}(3)(4) = 12$. 3 rectangles: $3(10) + 4(10) + 5(10) = 120$. Total: $12 + 120 = 132$.

Chapter 5

Section 5.1

1. Not statistical
2. Statistical
3. Statistical
4. Not statistical
5. Answers vary

Explanations

1. There is only one answer (Paris). It does not vary.

2. Different students have different numbers of pets. The answers vary.

3. Heights vary from student to student.

4 There is only one answer (56). It does not vary.

5 Any question whose answers change from person to person. Example: "How many minutes do you spend on homework?" Different students spend different amounts of time.

Section 5.2

1 Bunched together

2 Yes, 25

3 Around 23–24

4 Student B

Explanations

1 The values only range from 10 to 14 (range $= 4$). They are close to each other.

2 Most values are between 3 and 8. The value 25 is far from the rest.

3 Most values cluster near these numbers. The data is symmetric around the middle.

4 Student A's range is $13 - 10 = 3$. Student B's range is $30 - 2 = 28$. Student B's data is much more spread out.

Section 5.3

1 Mean $= 7$, Median $= 7$

2 Mean $= 16.25$, Median $= 16.5$

3 Mean $= 22.8$; not a good description

4 Mean drops from 87 to 79.2

Explanations

1 Mean: $(3+5+7+9+11) \div 5 = 35 \div 5 = 7$. Median: middle value is 7.

2 Mean: $(12+15+18+20) \div 4 = 65 \div 4 = 16.25$. Median: $(15+18) \div 2 = 16.5$.

3 $(2+3+4+5+100) \div 5 = 22.8$. Most values are around 2–5. The outlier 100 pulls the mean way up. The median (4) is more typical.

4 Original mean: $435 \div 5 = 87$. New mean: $475 \div 6 \approx 79.2$. The low score pulled the mean down.

› Section 5.4

1 16 | 2 $Q1 = 5$, $Q3 = 12$, IQR $= 7$ | 3 2.4 | 4 0 | 5 Team A

Explanations

1 $26 - 10 = 16$.

2 Lower half: $3, 5, 7 \rightarrow Q1 = 5$. Upper half: $10, 12, 14 \rightarrow Q3 = 12$. IQR: $12 - 5 = 7$.

3 Distances from 8: $4, 2, 0, 2, 4$. MAD: $(4+2+0+2+4) \div 5 = 12 \div 5 = 2.4$.

4 Every value equals the mean (10). All distances are 0. MAD $= 0$.

5 Team A range: $70 - 50 = 20$. Team B range: $100 - 20 = 80$. Team A's scores are much closer together, so they are more consistent.

› Section 5.5

1 Mode $= 8$ 2 16 responses; mode $=$ Green 3 72°F 4 19 5 Histogram

6 Frequency table

Explanations

1 6: 1, 7: 2, 8: 3, 9: 2, 10: 1. The mode is 8 (highest frequency).

2 $5 + 3 + 7 + 1 = 16$. Green has the highest count.

3 72°F has 4 dots, more than any other value.

4 $12 + 7 = 19$ students in the 80–89 and 90–100 bins.

5 With 500 data points, a dot plot would be too crowded. A histogram groups ages into intervals.

6 The data is categorical (fruit names), not numerical intervals. A frequency table counts each category. A histogram requires numerical bins.

> Section 5.6

1 50% 2 The lowest 25% of the data 3 $5, 8, 15, 24, 28$ 4 Team X is more consistent

5 Store B

Explanations

1 The box ($Q1$ to $Q3$) always contains the middle 50%.

2. Each whisker represents 25% of the data. The left whisker covers min to $Q1$.

3. Min $= 5$. $Q1$: median of $5, 8, 12 = 8$. Median $= 15$. $Q3$: median of $20, 24, 28 = 24$. Max $= 28$.

4. Same median, but Team X's middle 50% spans only 10 points vs. 30 for Team Y. Team X scores are clustered more tightly.

5. Store B: IQR $= 62 - 55 = 7$, range $= 18$. Store A: IQR $= 25$, range $= 60$. Store B has much tighter data.

Section 5.7

1. Mean $= 20$, range $= 10$
2. Median
3. Class A
4. Store A is more consistent
5. Not necessarily

Explanations

1. Mean: $100 \div 5 = 20$. Range: $25 - 15 = 10$. "The typical value is 20, and the data spans 10 units."

2. The outlier 50 pulls the mean to 11.5. Most values are around 6. The median (6) is more typical.

3. Higher median ($85 > 80$) and smaller IQR ($8 < 20$), so scores were higher and more consistent.

4. Both average \$400, but Store A's sales vary within \$200 while Store B's vary within \$600. Store A has steadier sales.

5. The sports use different scales. Soccer range 3 out of a mean of ≈ 2.6 is relatively large. Basketball range 30 out of a mean of 75 is relatively smaller. Comparing raw ranges across different scales can be misleading.

Section 5.8

1. Stem 1: 5 8; Stem 2: 2 4 7; Stem 3: 1 5
2. Median $= 24$, Range $= 20$
3. 10 data points; mode $= 63$
4. Median $= 86.5$

Explanations

1. Split each number: tens digit is the stem, ones digit is the leaf. List leaves in order.
2. 7 values. Middle (4th) value is 24. Range: $35 - 15 = 20$.
3. Count all leaves: $4 + 4 + 2 = 10$. The value 63 appears twice (the only repeat).
4. Stem 7: 2 8; Stem 8: 1 3 5 8; Stem 9: 0 2 5 8. Middle values (5th and 6th): 85 and 88. Median: $(85 + 88)/2 = 86.5$.

Great Job! Keep Learning with ViewMath!

Keep up the great work! Visit **viewmath.com/TX-Grade6** for free lessons, practice, and more.

Workbook

Scan Me

Step-by-Step

Scan Me

3 Practice Tests

Scan Me

5 Practice Tests

Scan Me

7 Practice Tests

Scan Me

10 Practice Tests

Scan Me

Math in 30 Days

Scan Me

Quizzes

Scan Me

uthor's Final Note

hope you enjoyed this book as much as I enjoyed writing it. Whether you are a student working through e material, a parent supporting your child's learning, or a teacher guiding your class, I have tried to make is book as clear and engaging as possible. I hope I have succeeded. If you have any suggestions for provement, please let me know. I would love to hear from you.

e accuracy of calculations is very important to me. We have done our best, but I also expect that I have ade some minor errors. Constant improvement is the name of the game. If you find any errors, please let e know. I will fix them in the next edition.

or students: Your learning journey does not end here. I have written a series of books to help you learn ath. Make sure you browse through them. I especially recommend workbooks and practice tests to help you epare for your exams.

or parents: Thank you for investing in your child's education. I encourage you to explore the companion sources available online to help support your child outside the classroom.

or teachers: Thank you for the invaluable work you do every day. I hope this book serves as a useful resource your classroom. Feel free to reach out if you have suggestions or would like to discuss how best to use this ok with your students.

also enjoy reading your reviews. If you have a moment, please leave a review on where you found this book. will help others find this book. If you have any questions or comments, please feel free to contact me at :nazari@ViewMath.com.

nd one last thing: Remember to use online resources for additional help. I recommend using the resources n `https://ViewMath.com`. You can find video lessons, practice problems, and more. You can also use the nline companion for this book to track your progress and access additional resources.

ishing all students the best in their studies, parents every success in supporting their children, and teachers ontinued inspiration in their classrooms!

r. A. Nazari

www.ingramcontent.com/pod-product-compliance
Ingram Content Group UK Ltd.
Pitfield, Milton Keynes, MK11 3LW, UK
UKHW051509290926
15471UKWH00008B/1508

9 798895 998649